BY
MADISON PATE

BRICK OF SOUND 4

BY
MADISON PATE

T&J PUBLISHERS

A SMALL INDEPENDENT PUBLISHER WITH A BIG VOICE

Printed in the United States of America by
T&J Publishers (Atlanta, GA.)
www.TandJPublishers.com

Cover design by Supply Graphics
Book format and layout by Timothy Flemming, Jr. (T&J Publishers)

ISBN: 979-8-218-38366-4

To contact author, go to:

Website: www.madison-pate.com
Email: contact@madison-pate.com
Facebook: Madison Pate
Instagram: Brick of Sound
LinkedIn: Madison Pate

This book is dedicated to my close friends in 2022.
There was no greater support system for me to
have at that time.

TABLE OF CONTENTS

Chapter 1

PRESENTING OCCUPATIONS

With acquired fame, comes acquired reputation. Now that the band has become famous through saving Single Town from a fierce foe, they now have a reputation to hold, thus the higher stakes. They gained a huge fan base throughout the world. People constantly are finding out more and more things about them, putting our tenor at the greatest risk. Once they find out about Power, things will go hectic.

Madison won't be able to do any of her moves without raising suspicion. Meaning she'll have to create a new name for her power.

But, that aside, let's go look at some others. Arriving at a building, with the name of 'Evil ~~Doer~~ Removal'. The 'Doer' was poorly drawn through, so this must be a suspicious business.

"First of all, Susan, we don't remove people who beat you in an argument on social media. Last, get your kids the health they deserve!" Kim shouted, slamming her hands down on her desk.

"My name isn't Susan, it's-" The lady began.

"I don't want to listen to what you have to say! Guards, escort her out of my office." Madison removed her from her chair, leaving her outside of the office and then shutting the door. She locked it, so she couldn't come back in. She began banging on the door.

"My husband is a lawyer, I can sue this c-"

"Shut the heck up and get out of this office before I get The Martinez!" Kim yelled, which finally compelled the lady to leave.

"Remember, if a hitman shows up, none of us are helping." Allie told Kim, who shrugged.

"Who gives a crap? We have those crystals, remember? You were the one who said that the person who grants the wishes doesn't care." Kim was brought up.

"But then there's the 'One's Beyond'!" Elizabeth said to her.

"They decide everything related to those things. They can destroy timelines, and everything is under their fingertips." Allie continued.

"Again, who cares. They said themselves that they don't care what we do, since ours is a lost cause. Earthland is the only dimension directly affected, and the others are indirectly affected by us." Madison agreed with Kim.

"Doesn't matter in the end. We need to stop criminals. Madison, go with Allie to find the one in that sketchy alleyway the other client was talking about."

Let's catch up with our beloved Bari.

"Come on kid, you're my successor, right? Try harder!" Ms. Martinez told Chloe, who picked up her Rainbow Sword. Stamina training was the main focus for today, so Ms. Martinez shot towards her for around the 1000th time.

Chloe blocked her first strike, then retaliated with a slash of her own.

"You're supposed to be my teacher, right? Try harder!" Chloe countered, parrying Ms. Martinez back to her spot. She wiped off some blood from the last slash. It had barely scraped her.

"This isn't comeback training. That's on Fridays! False Strike!" Using no energy whatsoever, she punched Chloe in the face, sending her flying into a nearby rock. After 1 year of training, she reverted her sun energy to nothing to use pure power. This form can last for 5 seconds, and can also lengthen her life span, as it was rapidly shortening, but steady due to her power regulator.

"Similar to a curse you're well familiar with, the original name for this technique is Zero." Ms. Martinez said, picking Chloe's sword off of the ground. She scanned it, looking at it like it was some form of toy. Chloe had practiced with it so much that it created a physical form. There were no scratches, gladly.

"How strong does this make the high schoolers?" Chloe asked, getting up off of the floor.

"Don't know, they improve at a rate faster than you guys. You know, the Big 3 could scale to some of them, but not even close to those Wind Ensemble members. Even making it in is tough. You would be better off making Symphonic Band, since that's as average as you could get." Ms. Martinez gave a very interesting answer, given how she is.

"...I see. They must have a great director, then." Chloe took her sword back, as Ms. Martinez gave her a thumbs up.

"'Course, it's Mr. Cook! Usually I remember the names of people if I fought them in the past, so that should say something!" Chloe made the sword vanish.

"That name does sound familiar." On the opposite side of this training area. Mandy was holding up a flame like shield, blocking all of Mrs. Staller' oncoming bullets. Once the piercing bullet appeared, Mandy summoned a flame hammer that enlarged to boost herself out of the way. Over the break, her weapon had been awakened. The basis of it is that the hammer can increase in size and weight, as well as decrease. It could be used as a jump spike.

Mandy is practicing for the main important events, but doesn't go along with everyday shenanigans. She is currently on a quest to find him.

"How's that will to live doing? I mean, your aura is blue." Mandy asked Mrs. Staller, who lowered her gun a bit.

"It helps me snipe better. The will to live can heighten either my senses or my dodges, and it boosted my senses. You see that rock over there?" She explained, pointing the gun at it. Mandy nodded, and right when she did so, she shot straight through the middle.

"That was around 400 meters away."

Meanwhile, in a corner store.

"That will be 5.98$. Cash or credit." James stated, behind the register.

"Can I pay with essential oils?" The lady from earlier questioned him, placing them all on the counter.

"No." James generated a wind blast to knock the bottles and the lady out of the door.

"That wasn't necessary at all." Walter told him, in a chair behind the counter. James looked at him.

"But the store policy said to kick out any scammers."

"You're supposed to kick them, not blast them."

Down in Single Town

While Madison was doing her side job, Mary filled in as president. After the war they got in earlier, all of the soldiers were put on cleaning duty, as the town was covered in mayonnaise.

"That stupid Mayo Cannon. Why the hell would you have one of those?" Mary thought, wiping some off of her desk.

"Yo, president! How's it going?" Ash asked her, walking in from the opened door. Mary glanced up at her.

"Oh, it's you. It's fine, I guess. That Bronze guy picked the wrong town to hit with a cannon. A Mayo Cannon of all things." Mary answered, motioning for her to sit down. Ash did so.

"I can see that. What's your next move?"

"Well, he's gone anyway. That tenor of ours got potential somewhere in that skull, or whatever's in her. Her bones are stronger than normal, and are hard to crack, even from my standards. She's the only one to break her bones." Mary put her feet up on the presidential desk, knocking over a wanted poster of herself.

"Maybe she isn't human." Ash brought up, joking.

"It would explain a lot, but it's not likely."

In The Alleyway

Madison lowered her hand, removing it from the face of the criminal she just slammed into the wall.

"You should be lucky that UR Tenor 2.0 isn't a Haste card. My Aggro deck is way better than your Mid-Range deck." Madison told Allie, putting her hands in her pockets.

"No way! You cheat with LR Tenor! She wipes the board! You don't even use an Aggro deck, you use a Domination deck!" Allie retaliated, as Madison laughed.

"Your deck just sucks so bad! Tuba Archetypes aren't going to save you! Try using more starters instead of the new releases!"

"Why would I use an old ca-" Madison put her hand over her mouth, then telling her to hush.

"There's a person nearby. Shut up!" Madison whisper shouted. They both looked in the direction where the light was stronger, and saw a bunch of rocks fly past it. They deadpanned in unison.

"It's her." They thought at the same time.

"Stupid criminals, thinking you can take my money. Who do you think I am?" Ms. Stevens exclaimed. Señora Salcedo arrived on the scene.

"Oh, I thought they were significant. *My bad.*" She walked away, giving Madison the chance to book it out of there, grabbing Allie's arm. Once she started jumping over buildings, Allie removed herself from the tenor.

"You scared of them or something?" She asked, as Madison pointed towards the ground.

"Remember, when we snuck out of the Band House, I wasn't supposed to leave because of my injury! When the battle was over, I managed to make it to my house, so they don't know where I am!" Madison responded, landing on the building that she worked at.

"I mean, they haven't looked for you yet. They must know, because it's very noticeable when you're gone." Allie said, landing.

"...what."

Chapter 2

FACING CONFLICT

Ah, yes. The state of Madison's life. Her power was extremely confusing, after realizing that the powers had fused together. Plus, she had to create a new naming scheme.

"How does 'Pow' sound?" Madison asked Kandi, walking through the street.

"Too obvious."

"Damn it! Alright, what about 'Er'?"

"Too sketchy." Madison marked off name after name in Orange Juice Recipes, not able to tell if any of them stuck.

"Oh, look who it is! That tenor from the band!" A figure shouted over to Madison, who glanced at them. She grabbed Kandi by the arm and threw her into the air.

"Aren't you that weird gang leader with that odd power? Only time I heard about you was back a year ago. But compared to me, you're on level zero!" She kicked him on the right side of his face, knocking him into a nearby wall.

Madison then caught Kandi in her arms.

"Any luck from that?"

"Yup." The rest of the Kelli Squad were moved into the band house, because their base was destroyed by Bronzeland. So, Madison had to be very careful when going places with her friends. This however, was her unlucky day.

"I have to make it in through the broken window, but it got fixed…!" Madison thought out loud, preparing to jump. A hand grabbed her shoulder, prompting her to turn to see who it was.

"Hello, daughter." Ms. Stevens told Madison, which sent strikes of fear down her spine.

"…crap." She brought the tenor into Ms. Martinez's office. The only thing that changed from it since she left was that a mission poster was taken down. The hero sighed.

"Madison, just because the band hasn't started back yet doesn't mean you can just straight up sneak out. Has your wound even healed?" Ms. Martinez asked her, as Madison nodded.

"This is the second time I remember you being blasted in the stomach, which was both technically by yourself." Ms. Stevens told Madison.

"But those were completely situational losses! Just like my other fights. I've never won anything before. Wait, I'm getting off track! What were we talking about again?" Madison questioned them.

"I'm trying to have a serious conversation here." Ms. Martinez thought.

"We were talking about you sneaking out. Explain yourself." Ms. Stevens answered.

"Oh, yeah! Well, you see, I couldn't leave Single Town by itself without its president! Even when I'm in terrible shape, I have to do my job! With the exception of my legs being burned." Madison added on.

"Your power center is severely damaged, you know. Keep this up, and you'll be in the same situation as me." Ms. Martinez told Madison, who shrugged.

"Situation, smituation, I'm the cool, epic tenor. Worst that could happen is the rest of my body was lit on fire!" She began to get up, but she was stopped by the similar gravity effect used against her during the practice hero exams.

"You need to get a grip on reality, 2.0. Just because you lost a few times doesn't mean you're going to win now, especially with that injury." Ms. Martinez then released the gravity effect, which got Madison to get up and open the door.

"Yeah, you're right. Everything else I've done, I've failed at. Avenging my master, saving the Epitomus people, and a whole lot of other things. I'm *supposed* to be the prestigious tenor..." She began to get shaken up.

"...but I can't even scratch the surface of something I practiced for for months. I placed my expectations so high, and now it's my fault that I don't like how it turned out." She shut the door, walking back up to her room. She sat down on her bed, looking at the tenor case next to her door.

"Saxophone Salad, you're always there for me. What should I do?" Madison asked the case, but it didn't give its typical glow.

"I'd advise on thinking it over. Perhaps a trip to your town would work?" Saxophone Salad responded.

"Huh, that's a good idea." The Power user then stood up, picking up the case. "Wait, you can talk? How cool is that?"

"All cursed instruments have souls, and I just so happened to awake today. Good day, owner." They responded, the green glow coming off.

"Huh, you must sleep for a while. Well, thanks for the recommendation! I'm going to go to bed now." She placed the saxophone back in its original spot, and went to lay down on her bed. Staring at her ceiling meant it was time to ponder on her future as a hero.

"My legs won't be healed completely, so those burns are probably here to stay." Madison thought, then wincing in pain from remembrance of that day. She couldn't breathe because of the ash and almost passed out right when she woke up again. Those months where she couldn't stand. Sometimes, she could still smell the lingering of her burnt blood.

"Hey, Madison...?" A voice said from behind her door. The tenor immediately shot up, running to the door. When she opened it, the person there was Kandi.

Huh. That's weird. Shouldn't she be at the original Band House? Why was she here this late at night?

"Yeah? What's up?" Madison backed up, letting her close the door behind her.

"Do you know where Allie is? I have to ask her a question."

"The room on the right."

"Alright, thanks. I'll see you later then." The section leader suddenly had the urge to go to sleep. She yawned, then waved her off.

"Good night." Everything she heard soon after was really hazy, but it felt close to her. It seemed like it was outside of her head, instead of inside like the alter egos she used to have.

"...see...one...works...how...last..."
What?

A sensation of warmth washed over the manifestation of Madison in her own head in the form of a light breeze. She closed her eyes to feel the sudden pleasantness of how this felt. Instead of the bleak, pitch black area she was used to, that occasionally had water at the floor, along came a garden of sorts. The green grass, the bright sun, that blue sky. Opening her eyes, the tenor bent down to pick up a stray flower pedal.

"The you that is normally in control has gone to sleep, so I have taken over. You may find things that pique your interest in this peaceful land." A voice deeper than her own told her.

So this is where you reside, huh? She asked this voice, curious to know where they came from.

"As like Power World, this place is only a figment of your imagination. A dream, is that what you Earthland beings call it?"

Yeah. Huh, Power World wasn't real? That's interesting.

"As it's from your imagination, any information I can give you at the time is limited in this world. But, as I am you, and you are me, this doesn't stop from you seeing things from my cognition as well. I have existed as long as Power has seen the light of day. I am the side effect of the creation of such a thing." They elaborated further.

Let me ask you one thing before I look around. What's going on out there? Is it something I should worry about?

"Nothing of your immediate concern, I suppose. Do not worry, I've already handled everything. For a human, I used to think that you were actually quite incompetent-"

How rude of you! I'll be seeing my lawyer about this. Madison interrupted. The voice sighed, not proud of her antics.

"But since you can finally hear my voice, I think it's time you come to the truth. You won't remember much when you awake, but there's some things that you need to see in this land."

Chapter 3

POWER TO ZERO

The tenor awoke from her slumber, kind of sort of remembering a weird dream she had. It didn't feel like a dream when she was having it, but now it feels like one. Something involving plants, apparently.

But no matter, it was time she headed to her favorite place on Earth.

They arrived at the shore near Single Town, the one where they captured Future Madison at. Kim looked at her watch. Right when it turned 12:00, a taxi pulled up at the shore. The driver rolled down the window, revealing Junior.

"You guys in need of service?" He asked, as Madison laughed.

"Not that kind of service. We need to get to Couple Town." Madison explained to him.

"Then get in your seats. It'll be super fast!" Once they got there, they stepped out.

"So, aside from the...mayo...what else has changed about this place?" Madison questioned Junior, making sure to step over it while walking.

"There's this underground base under the coffee shop that we just can't open." He told the group.

"It must need the power of the Criminal Remover Kim!" Kim exclaimed.

"Nope. Definitely not." Allie and Junior said in sync.

"Usually, when something can't be opened, Madison could just open it! You should give it a try." Elizabeth said while patting Madison's shoulder.

"Good point, trumpet! Wait a minute. Underground base..." Madison agreed, as Junior brought them to the coffee shop. He opened up the hidden door that was on the floor, which led to a staircase.

"I've seen this place before. I wonder when," Allie thought, choosing to walk in first, having everyone else go behind her. Once they reached the door, Madison placed her hand on the wall scanner next to it. It opened up the door, reminding the tenor of the place.

"Those blueprints! Allie, do you have them?" Madison asked Allie, and luckily she did.

"Alright, what secret info does it have hidden?" All Elizabeth did was lightly tap the blueprints, and all of the information was put on display in the demon language by some sort of high level technology. If the government had this 100 years ago, imagine what the people could've had by now.

"It says 'Prototype Zero. Status: Failed. Termination By: Project One.'" The one quick enough to notice was Elizabeth.

"Madison, I've connected all of the dots, so excuse this very long dialogue space." She told the tenor, who nodded in approval.

"Alright, it says terminated by Project One. Epitomus Allie worked for the government in some capacity, and she mind controlled Karla, which got your legs burned. Which in turn means," She waited for anyone to finish.

"You're Prototype Zero!" Kim exclaimed, gaining a high five from the trumpet. Madison was eating a piece of bread she had brought with her.

"Nice." Allie slapped her across the face, which got her back to her senses.

"Wait, if this is where we found Project Xenos, which started 100 years ago...Then that makes me Xenos, the creator of all powers?" Madison asked them.

"Yeah. That means you have the ability to learn any ability you desire, but since you're put in a very realistic mechanical body..." Allie began.

"There might be a limit to that. But don't worry, we've seen a lot of powers, so any you chose will be yours to keep. Your powers, all three of them, have combined to make the balance of all things! The first power created in 10,000 years, and you get to choose the name!" She explained, gaining nods from the tenor from throughout the way. Madison pointed her bread at the princess.

"Of course, I'm choosing the name Zero. Three reasons. It's technically my name, it's a part of this song called Zero to One, and with the combination of my powers, I'm on level zero."

"Wait a minute, isn't that bread fro-" Kim was interrupted by Madison running out of the door, opening it with her hand.

"There's still that criminal we have to deal with! Come on!"

In the Band House Extended

There's no S-Rank missions anymore. In turn, that means two things. One, they don't have anything to worry about regarding money, and 2, they have less room to improve. That also means they could focus more on band related things instead of hero related ones, giving them a break.

"How's the hero exams doing? I know they haven't started yet, but are they prepared?" Ms. Stevens asked Ms. Martinez.

"Yeah. Since the Big 3 have to do the ones for their pro licences, then maybe not them. They have to work way harder than I did. The exams are gonna be on the big screen, broadcasted everywhere this time! Plus, the Band Festival is gonna be huge! We need to start recording the introductions." Ms. Martinez answered.

"Introductions?"

In Single Town

They caught the criminal, and Madison dropped them off in front of her desk in the presidential office. Mary looked down at them.

"They've been stealing burgers." Kim explained. Once Mary got a closer look, she finally figured out who it was.

"I thought I told you to stay in your burger place on the outskirts between Single Town and Couple Town, not here!" She exclaimed. He had smoke coming off of him, because he was just blasted by one of Elizabeth's fireworks.

"I wanted to see what was going on here, you know, with the mayo cannon!" He responded.

"Jeez. If you just wanted to see the mayo cannon, you could've come with me to Bronzeland. But you declined!"

Junior told him, lifting him off of the ground.

"Oops. Well, there's no point in it now." Junior took him outside, leading him to the underground base they had set up.

"So, faithful disciple, what plans do you have outside of Single Town?" Mary asked the tenor, who shrugged.

"Aside from Symphonic Camp in a few days, nothing. Mainly because of my ungodly luck." Madison told her.

"It's the worst month in Single Town history. The worst month ever!" Kim complained.

"Oh, yeah. February. I hate February." Madison blandly stated.

"Well, for Couple Town, February is the best month." Allie remarked.

"No one asked." Kim and Madison countered at the same time. They continued to playfully bicker for a while until they eventually split up in the office. Kim spoke to Mary about some strange plan she had in the works to get 'a whole lot of fame', in her words. Allie took the chance to familiarize herself with her friend's workspace. It's not every day that they're allowed the chance to come down here to manage their towns. Surprisingly, Madison's desk was clean, and only had a few strange papers littered about. There were a few picture frames, most of which including the two of them together.

"Aww! I didn't know you had these!" She picked up one. It was from their first B Class Mission together, taken selfie style from courtesy of yours truly. The tenor was caught off guard, so she wasn't exactly looking at the camera at the moment. "Honestly, I expected to see more of Chloe or even *Mandy* here. You guys were closer first..." Madison had a faint look of embarrassment.

"You're my closest friend. Those two have Brandon to fight all the time. It's only fair I can get someone that's on my level too." For a second, she didn't recognize Allie's expression. Though, it quickly turned to a *very* giddy one, as the girl ran over to Madison to give her a tight hug.

"You have *no* idea how much this means to me!" It didn't take long for her to relax in Allie's embrace. "Don't feel left out. Not just from them, but you're not the only one with a bunch of pictures on your desk. I think I have some of these ones myself." She chuckled, gaining a small smile in response.

"Yet I still can't see, even though you've seen my whole office?" Madison was banned from Couple Town, even though her best friend was the president for christ's sake. The 'not' demon princess was first to let go.

"Nope. Not until I get everything together."

....

Character Introduction: Mandy

"Uh, is the thing working?" Mandy asked.

"Yeah, you can start." Ms. Martinez responded, placing the camera down on a stand.

"Okay, hello I guess. I'm Mandy, section leader of the oboes. I'm Sky Human, and considering that, you may be asking about my wings. They aren't there, end of story."

"Wow, you can't just immediately shut them down. Moving onto the next one, I guess."

"Fine. I'm interested in fighting and winning. I also prioritize my oboe reeds over people. They're way too expensive. Too much."

"Alright, where do you work?"

"I don't work anywhere, and I'm keeping it that way.

The only job I need to do is beat him, once and for all."

"Your final goal?"

"To become number one. Nothing else but that will make me finally happy."

"And what's your ideal hero?"

"The one who always wins, no matter what."

Chapter 4

ANOTHER ENCOUNTER

Finally, after the trial and error of the hero trials, combined with the moon and the city of gold, we've finally arrived at Symphonic Camp. Where our heroes will acquire knowledge for HGPE that isn't from Ms. Martinez. It's also the point in time where the paths of the 7th graders and the 8th graders will collide. There must be a big difference to how they act, right? Let's see what Madison is up to.

"We're gonna hit that wall thing over there! Slow down!" She exclaimed, on an empty chair rack along with Allie. Alex was pushing it, with no sign in slowing down. Before they hit the wall, it came to an abrupt stop, with Alex activating his platinum. The force that was shot back towards him was negated by it.

"Close call." Allie hopped off of the rack. Madison did so also, mimicking her under her breath.

"We need to get back to the band room and practice." This sparked a memory in Madison's head.

"Oh, we're meeting that high school director today. What was his name…? Mr. Cook? I swear it sounds so familiar." Madison stated, walking back down the hallway, with the other two close behind her.

"You aren't wrong. It's very familiar, like we've met him before or something." A pressure came down on the three of them, almost bringing them to the ground. They were strong enough to stay up, and Madison turned around to see who it was.

"You guys must be 8th graders! My name is Mr. Cook, the high school band director." Mr. Cook introduced himself. The pressure was released, giving them a sense of relief.

"Thought we were being attacked by a villain or something. The name's Madison, the tenor." Madison introduced herself to him.

"Wait, you're the daughter of The Martinez, right? Member of the Big 3?" He asked Allie, who made a smug face to Madison, then turned back to him.

"Yeah, in the flesh."

"I've heard a lot about you from her. She says you have your hero license and everything. That's cool."

"Speaking of heroes, what's your ranking?" Alex questioned him.

"If Ms. Martinez dies, I will become the number one hero."

....

The throne wars. The war of the best. There's multiple terms for it. Whoever wins this war after the number one falls, wins the title of number one hero. With this acquired fame, they win the world. That's at least how it happens normally. But now, they just have a replacement. Someone they've never met before.

"This won't do anything but destroy the kids' dreams. If we don't do the wars, it just won't be-" Señora Salcedo began, then was stopped by Ms. Martinez.

"Sorry, but this has to be done. Government's orders. Maybe next time we'll-" Ms. Martinez was interrupted by a rock almost hitting her in the face, but stopping before it did.

"You really think we're doing this for the government? No! It's for the kids, it's for the school, it's for the band, it's for us! The people need us now!" Ms. Stevens told her, as the rock fell.

"There won't be a next time for those kids. Don't you remember? Because of the government's orders, the school system is shutting down so we can focus on hero work, and you didn't want to do that! So what's wrong with us wanting to do the throne wars?"

"She has a point, Maria. If you didn't want to listen to them before, why listen to them now?" Ms. Martinez thought about it for a minute.

"Fine, then. We'll still host the throne wars, but he has to participate." Ms. Martinez decided.

"I guess we can all agree on that." Señora Salcedo told her, and Ms Stevens nodded.

....

"Number one, huh. Ain't that special. Well, we've got to get to sectionals, so it's time for us to leave." Madison walked off, leaving the three behind.

"Don't you want to learn more about it? Don't you have that *ambition* too?" Mr. Cook questioned her, the word emphasized sending chills through Madison's body.

"Ambition, shmambition. None of my business anymore. I've lost all interest." Thankfully, the path to their assigned room wasn't that far. Her footsteps echoed in the hallway, aided by the silence between the two. There was something off about him…but Madison couldn't put a finger on it, so she just kept it pushing. There were a few students hanging around in the hallways. All of them were in clumps of groups except for Bailey and Aaliyah. The two were nowhere near the Low Reeds' assigned room, instead looking at some paper the two shared. They spoke in a low whisper to each other. All Madison could see on the flyer with a glance was a hexagon like symbol along with some text. "…Uh. What is that?" She approached them. The two frantically looked for a way to hide the paper, with Bailey deciding to tear the thing to shreds.

"Just s-some dumb high school club trying to recruit us. Never too early to start finding prospective members, right?" She didn't stutter often. Normally, Bailey was composed enough to be able to find a way to insult Madison specifically on the spot. To get her point across, she slammed her foot down on Aaliyah's.

"Y-Yeah, yeah! That's right." She winced from the pain. Well…if they didn't want to tell her, then it wasn't any of her business. Madison simply blinked in response, walking past them.

· · · · · · · · · · · · · · · · ·

Character Introduction: Amy

"Let's just get this over with. I'm Amy, flute section leader. I'm a full blooded human. All I like to do is destroy things with explosions. I work as a flute traveler, collecting money by defeating wanted criminals around the world. My final goal is to become the number one hero, so people become more intimidated by me. The ideal hero should never run away!" Amy answered all of the questions without Ms.

Martinez speaking.

"...I wasn't even recording." Ms. Martinez told her, which caused Amy to give off a bit of her aura.

"Are you serious?" She asked angrily.

"No."

Chapter 5

WHAT'S WILLPOWER?

Symphonic Camp went well for our band. They met their underlings, and they got along well. Mr. Cook was struck with mixed emotions from the 8th graders. Some thought he was cool. Some thought he was sketchy. Some thought he was crazy. Multiple opinions. On this fabulous Monday, they were excused from their first few classes for a big lesson for the 8th graders.

"Today we will be learning about alignments." Ms. Martinez proudly stated, standing on her podium.

"Instrument alignments?" Madison questioned her, upside down on her chair.

"No, sit up. We're learning about what your energy says about you. For example, Allie. Come up here." Ms. Martinez elaborated, as Madison shifted herself in her spot. Once Allie got up there, Ms. Martinez placed her hand on her head.

"So, do any of you know what color her aura is?"

"Black and red." The ones who could answer said.

"Now, what's her alignment?" The room went completely silent, for once in their lives.

"Okay, this is going to be harder than I thought. There's three wills. The will to fight, will to survive, and the will to conquer. The will to fight can do things like either boost your fighting spirit to immense levels or allow you to use invisible armor. The will to survive can either give you anything similar to the ability to see attacks coming more often or let you perfectly counter attacks. Then finally, the will to conquer." Ms. Martinez explained, then sighing. This usually wasn't a talkable topic, but she knew she could do it.

"Anyone suited to rule any place is considered a conqueror. I myself have the will to conquer, and a few of you guys could possibly have it. It gives you two of the perks that the other wills give you. Completely randomized, too. I can just barely see into the future to dodge and I've got the fighting spirit."

The Will to Fight: The main techniques that are possible to have are Spirit Boost, Aura Armor, and Emission. Spirit Boost can drive your own will to fight, and can make you a bit stronger also. Aura Armor is the user's aura, which is invisible, comes out and acts as an enhancer. It boosts endurance and power. Emission is the advanced form of Aura Armor, which can project it out from around the user's body. Other unnamed forms are possible.

The Will to Survive: The main techniques that are possible to have are Prediction, Aura Sight, and Perfect Counter. Prediction is the ability to possibly predict your opponent's attacks and to know what's coming. Aura Sight allows the user to make out who's who by just their aura, and can see it from a long distance. Perfect Counter is the advanced form of Aura Sight, which allows some to, as the name suggests, perfectly counter attacks with the same strength output. Other unnamed forms are possible.

"And what do you expect for us to do with this informa-tion?" Mandy asked, leaning on the wall near the drumset. Ms. Martinez pointed outside the window towards the almost empty field.

"Figure it out with each other."

15 Minutes Later

"That was easy. All I did was fight you, and now I'm pumped for more!" Allie shouted over to Madison, who pointed her arm towards her, charging a blast.

"You want to fight more? I'm perfectly fine with that. Tenor Neck Zero!" The blast began in a normal line, but it began curving in an S-shape, until finally landing, releasing smoke.

"Interesting attack." Allie summoned the trident and charged towards Madison, trying to stab her. On instinct, Madison picked up a music stand off of the ground and blocked all of the incoming strikes.

"Thrust Zero: 1 Pin!" Attempting at striking an important point, Madison spun it around to use the back part of it to land the hit. It missed, so she used it as a distraction to get the trident away.

"Let's see. I have to exploit any of my opponents weak points, but that's dishonorable. What should I do...?" Allie thought.

"Having trouble, demon princess? You're supposed to be the next number one but you can't think of a plan on the spot!" Red bolts of lightning came out of her fist, but instead of using it to hit her, she used her leg. A typical Madison move.

"You suck!" Allie grabbed Madison's leg and threw

her at a tree. Meanwhile, the alto William was just standing around.

"It isn't hard. I've always known that I could perfectly counter." He said.

"William, no one cares." Another alto, Chimera told him. Chloe was attempting to slice a tree. She could do it at ease with her rainbow sword, but she wants to see if she could do it with her hands.

"Focus on my willpower. I've got to focus on it." Chloe thought on and on. She imagined a small flame in her mind, attempting to grab hold of it. Once she did, she got a vision. The figures were blurry, and also hard to hear.

"You can't kill me! Your childish mind isn't strong enough!" A voice shouted. Without hesitation from the other figure, they drove a weapon through them.

"What was that? I'm not a child. I'm a hero." The voice faded to nothing, along with the vision to black. When she returned to her senses, five trees were already cut down. Chloe had awakened her will to fight.

"That's certainly a way to do things." Mandy dodged all of the lightning bolts from James. He trained himself to be able to do them constantly. Mandy was able to see the exact time period when it was shot and dodge accordingly. It wasn't perfect, though. She could only dodge 1/5 of the attacks.

"I wish I could move as fast as these guys, be as strong, and be as confident. Bombs don't work against villains." Kim said, sitting on a rock.

"You want to be number one, right? Then stand up and figure your alignment out! Maybe you have something completely different from everyone else!" Elizabeth told Kim, so she listened.

"Oh yeah, by the way, there's two other things. Color of Perception and Color of Command! Conquers have command on default, but it's possible to have perception. Perception gives you the ability to have your senses unaltered by anything. For example, conversations can be heard clearly if it's going on close to you. If you focus on a person, you could see their aura and be able to tell weak points. Close your eyes, and imagine people as blobs of energy!" Ms. Martinez explained again, watching over everyone from a tree.

Kim did so. It wasn't that fine tuned, but she could see at least the outlines of the aura. Her senses would slowly be heightened to that of a mythical power holder. Gradually over time, due to her not having a power, this perception would help her fight. But, that won't be happening for a while. She has a business to uphold. A reputation, if you will.

"I still don't have anything flashy like Chloe. Nothing useful like Madison. Like, there's a few other powerless people here that I know of, but they're monsters compared to me!" Kim described. Ms. Martinez grabbed her face, taking her out of her possibly endless monologue.

"You have dreams! Ambition! You can't just let your dreams be destroyed because you don't have powers! Think of the people who did have powers and lost ambition!"

....

Madison sat on the couch in the Band House Extended, staring down at her hands. She was starting to get scars from overusing her power concentrated moves.

"So, aside from working for Evil Remover, what else do you do?" Kim asked Madison, who glanced over to her.

"Just sit around and think of all of the things I've done wrong. All of the things I've failed. All of the things I've lost." At the last sentence she clenched her fists.

"Madison, quit sulking. We've got your point already. You think you're bad at everything." Allie told her, while playing

Tenor Adventures.

"I don't just think I'm bad! I am bad! How many times have I actually won something or done something or...!" Before she could continue shouting, she walked out of the house, slamming the door behind her.

"What's gotten into her?" Chloe questioned, reading a newspaper.

"After seeing the light when she came back to us, she's gotten visions of past events. Mainly when she got burned. It didn't affect her then, so I guess the light triggered it."

....

Madison picked up the stand again, thinking of it as a weapon. When Allie charged towards her again, she stuck it into the ground, and used it as an escape ticket upwards.

"Drop Kick Zero!" Madison kicked Allie into the ground, then picked the stand back up when she landed.

"You should get that modified so you can use it to fight." Kendall told her, walking over to Madison. The tenor tossed the stand to the bassoon.

"Good idea."

"Madison, are you still going to become number one? Or did you chicken out?" Allie questioned her, getting up out of the ground.

"No way I chickened out! I'm going to be so strong in the future that no one else will be able to beat me in a fight!"

"Well, you're going to have to toughen up!" Allie blasted Madison with the demon energy. Madison held up her hand, and awakened some form of power, because she absorbed the entire thing.

"...what?"

Character Introduction: James

"I'm James, the ex-Darklands Prince, section leader of the Clarinets. I like working at my job at the corner store near the Hero Stadium, because I get paid 30 an hour." He began.

"30 an hour for a corner store?" Ms. Martinez questioned him.

"Wanted criminals come in sometimes."

"Okay. Continue."

"I want to become number one so I can show the Darklands King that I am the rightful successor. The ideal hero is someone who could defeat villains on their own."

"So without the rest of the Big 3?"

"I can fight without them, just not against a big threat like him."

Chapter 6

ANGER RELEASE

The great tale of the great royal demon family line. An ability can be passed down to the next prodigy of the line. Of course, the only demon left was Allie. Well, half demon.

"I need to turn people into stone!" Allie shouted, trying to turn Madison into stone.

"Well, it's not working on me. All it's doing is giving me a horrible headache." She responded, clutching her head.

"I could turn him to stone just fine!" Allie pointed at Walter, who had half of his body in stone.

"And I could only stop it with my time control just in time to cover half of me." He said.

"So it's preventable by a specific kind of force. That force is possible to be broken, but there's some that can't be destroyed." Madison mumbled while writing notes down in 'Orange Juice Recipes.'

"Like what? It affects the soul directly, which means

you could be affected."

"I don't know, but my soul is protected from evil princesses like you!" Madison explained, closing the notebook shut.

"What did you call me, bucket man?" Allie asked her, charging her blasts.

"I don't know, what did I call you, crap leader?"

"Hey, you can at least release me from the stone. I have a job." Walter told Allie, trying to break through it with his hand.

"Sure." With the simple snap of a finger, he was released from the stone. So, he went on with his day, walking off.

"Can I go home now? It's the time when I sit and stare in my room." Madison asked Allie, beginning to walk away. The demon princess grabbed her shoulder.

"From now on, you can't just sit around in your room when you're not doing your job! What's there to be sad about, you have practically the most overpowered power!"

"Everything! I can't do anything, but I'm expected to! Just because I have the most overpowered power doesn't mean I'm the most overpowered person! No one understands that!" Madison responded, then swiping away the hand on her jacket.

"Madison." Allie started, which made the tenor look back at her from over her shoulder.

"...what?"

"*I* understand."

Flashback Begin

"Come on, Karla, listen to me! Can't you just snap out of it?" Madison cried out, backing up on the cliff.

She was far enough from Karla to not be affected by her Flames of Hell technique. It was a power up that set the area around her on fire.

"I don't know who you are. Aside from my target." EP Allie said through Karla, but it came out as the latter's voice. Madison reached the edge of the cliff, not daring to look how far down it was. She resorted to getting into her fighting stance.

"Now's not the time to start speaking nonsense! Why aren't you listening to me?" Madison shouted over to Karla, who quickened her walking pace.

"I am, it's just that I can't control my body!" Karla thought, trying to stop EP Allie. But she was simply not strong enough to do so. The wind of the flames burned off part of Madison's pants, up to her knees.

"Here goes nothing!" Madison thought, then jumping backwards as a way of escape. Karla extended her flames far enough to grab hold of Madison's legs.

Red. All Madison could see was red. The pain in her legs were immense, easily some sort of degree burns. She knew somehow she was barely standing. All she could feel was the pain in her legs, combined with the blood coming down it.

"What are you, a monster? You were just a level two threat, nowhere near five!" EP Allie yelled over to her, as the evil aura took over Madison. Irregular black lines spread all throughout her body, starting from her feet.

"I'm your worst nightmare." A voice, not Madison's, retaliated. Ms. Martinez arrived on the scene, while carrying the bandaged Mandy and Chloe. They decided to watch from afar.

"That's going to scar her for the rest of her life."

Ms. Martinez thought. Using the dark energy, Madison blasted Karla. It didn't hurt her, but all it did was remove EP Allie from her body.

"Hopefully that annoyance is gone…" She trailed off, then falling sideways onto the ground. Madison was now completely passed out.

"It had to be the legend." Mandy said, and Chloe agreed.

"Yeah, Negative Drive."

Flashback End

Madison was now where the waterfall was, surrounding the part of her body in water in a bubble, so she wouldn't have to worry about drying it off later. The only part of her body out of the water was her nose and up.

"Why're you helping me? Your efforts won't change a thing." Madison asked Allie, who was watching her stare off into the distance ahead.

"Because if I can't help you, then no one can. Go on, release your anger." She answered.

"I can't just do it on command. I have to be in the wrong situation at the right time."

"Think of everything that ruined your life. The reason why all you do outside of school is just do nothing but be unproductive!"

"That's not true!" Allie didn't know if to say this or not, but she had to for the sake of getting Madison back to her senses.

"Then say that to your master! They left you because of how much of an idiot you are!" The tenor paused for a bit to process the comment. Madison got out of the water, somehow learning to stand on it.

"Take that back!" Madison exclaimed. Since it didn't work, Allie had one last shot to get in.

"I will once your master comes back!" The evil aura of Negative Drive bursted out, swirling around her in a spiral. Her eyes turned red. The same red that she saw that day. The yell that she let out had two voices to it. One was Madison, and the other was of whatever was inside her.

In Madison's mind, which was still the water, Madison was coughing up blood. The water had almost turned a red color. Triumphing over her, was herself.

"I'm now in control! Say goodbye to your life!" The tenor took the opportunity to kick her counterpart down to the ground.

"The only place my emotions get me is back in the same spot I began in!" Madison stood up, smirking down to her other self. Almost a shadow to herself.

"You know what, old loser? You should infuse your powers into mine, since I just beat you and all."

....

Character Introduction: Sid

"I'm Sid, a previous member of the darkland royal guard, and the section leader of the saxophones. I do intel missions by working with villains until they die." Sid introduced.

"Okay, Australia." Ms. Martinez said.

"What?"

"Just a nickname I thought of. Continue."

"I want to become the number one hero so everyone will bow down to me for once! The ideal hero has to never lose a fight!"

Chapter 7

THE MASK

Madison sighed, now alone in her mind. She doesn't have any issue with the others, but she prefers peace and quiet.

"Back to my roots. All alone." Her spirit chains were wrapped around her hands. Which means she's trapped. Not in her mind, but with herself. Before she could continue monologuing, Allie kicked her out of her trance.

"So underwhelming! I told you to release your anger! You got me so prepared to fight, then you just stood there! What's with y-" Allie was cut off by Madison putting her hand in her face.

"I found out something! Drive Two is fueled on fear, Drive Three is fueled on sadness, and now I figured out Drive Four!" Madison explained, then getting back on land.

"It's like you have a new drive for each book."

"What book? Allie, you're going crazy again." The tenor crossed her arms. Allie returned back to land also.

"Sure, you may have unlocked another section of the characters, but have you gotten all of their moves?"

"Yeah, good point. I have to think of another naming scheme." Ms. Martinez walks up to the both of them, holding up a fairly new looking mission post. It read: "S Class Mission: The Underworld's Mask".

"Great timing, then. We're returning to the Darklands. Word has it that there's a new prince." Ms. Martinez explained.

"A prince? Really? Well, we've got to go right away!" Allie responded, walking in the direction of the Band Houses.

"Hey, just because you're lovestruck doesn't mean you can make the decisions! Get back here!" Madison shouted, following her.

"What if he's my knight in shining armor?" She fantasized.

"What if he looks like Kim?" The tenor mocked.

"That'll cost you 15 gold coins."

"The heck? I ain't paying you so much money for a joke! Cut the crap!" Meanwhile, at Evil Remover, Kim was signing a paper.

"You sure you want to do this?" Elizabeth asked her. The clarinet finished writing her signature.

"If it means I get power, I'll sign this contract with the soul." Kim answered, as the soul of Saxophone Salad was floating in the chair across from her.

"So, where do we start?" They questioned Kim, who kicked back in her chair in an attempt at looking cool.

"When we head back to the Darklands, I want you to take control over my body, and use your soul powers to try and awaken them."

"This seems like a very bad idea. What if you don't have any powers to awaken?"

"Well, if Madison can awaken powers out of nowhere, then I should do that too!" At the corner store, Walter closed the shop.

"So we're closing early for the mission?" He asked James, who nodded.

"That mask is a big deal."

Arriving in the Darklands

"We're wanted dead here you know, why did we have to come back?" Kim questioned, frightened to even step out of the ship. Madison walked out at ease.

"Even if we don't remember what happened, the king probably twisted everything." She answered, now able to walk out without being blasted.

"She's right. That's something the king would do." James stated. Kendall went outside to go to the main town with Madison.

"Here's your weapon." He said, tossing a small canister towards her. Madison caught it, looking at it. It had the letter 'T' on it in blue.

"I appreciate the work, bassoon man, but how do I get it to work?" She wondered.

"Throw it on the ground. Go on, try it!" He told her. The tenor threw it on the ground as hard as she could, and it exploded. Once the smoke cleared, it revealed a music stand. It had a grip where Madison could hold it, and it looked shinier than before.

"I put a coat of my finest material around it, so it now has the best durability around! The only thing that could snap it is someone who's a universe buster!" He over-exaggeratedly explained, as Madison picked it up.

"So, it basically has no chance of being destroyed. Got

it. Come on, son! Let's head to town!" When they arrived, the first thing they noticed was that there were no guards. The town was completely deserted. The only thing left moving was a piece of paper. It was completely silent aside from the wind blowing. Has the city become a ghost town?

"Oh look, a wanted poster! For 500 gold? That's a lot!" Kendall said, grabbing it out of the air. The photo on it was...

Ms. Martinez.

"We've truly struck *gold*. Haven't we, bassoon man?" Madison chuckled, and the bassoon in question agreed.

"All we have to do is invade the pala-" Kendall was interrupted by the noise of metal hitting the top of a building in front of the two.

"What business do you foolish Earthlanders have to do with the Darklands?" The figure asked them. Though in the darkness of the Underworld, the radiance of the armor was still able to be seen. The weapon was a trumpet, along with an actual sword.

"Allie was right, he literally is a knight in shining armor," Madison thought, covering her eyes from the almost blinding light.

"I'm a mechanic, and definitely not foolish." Kendall responded to him. The figure dropped to the ground, of similar elegance to the king, but more than the previous prince.

"Show me your ruler, or we have a duel to the death." The figure told them. Kendall led him in the direction of the ship, leaving Madison to wander around.

"Great minds think alike." She laughed a little, going into the forest. There were three stops to make, to get clues to the whereabouts of the mask.

"Yes?" Roxy asked, opening up the door to see Madison.

"Yo! Do you guys know where the Mask of the Underworld is?" The tenor walked in, sitting down in the chair.

"In the heart of town." Gage answered, now with his new TV.

"Where the sun shines." Jonny also answered. Madison got up, and ran out.

"Thanks!" She arrived at her next stop, wasting no time to kick down the door.

"Where's the mask?" Madison shouted, her yell echoed throughout the mostly empty space.

"Down the stairs!" Maddie exclaimed back, so the tenor put the door back, then ran away. Meanwhile, outside the ship, the knight in the night was confused.

"What is this sorcery?" He asked Kendall, looking at the ship from multiple angles.

"It's called a spaceship. It can go into space, as well as other dimensions." The mechanic explained to him. Kim and Bailey were quick to understand otherworldly technology with the help of James, but the armored person was newer to the game.

"What's a dimension...?" Kendall patted his back.

"I feel bad for you man. Since you asked to see our ruler or whatever, how about we get you inside first." On the opposite side of town, Madison arrived at her final destination.

"Hey, you! Where's the Mask of the Underworld?" She shouted through the door. This was the residence of a person who she knew a while back. His name, she couldn't remember. He randomly disappeared when Allie went on that space trip, and they never saw him again. The two of them certainly had...*something* going on.

"Where the fun dies!" The person shouted back, leading Madison to her final conclusion.

"Thanks!" Madison ran into town, finding the building that stood out the most. It was presumably the new palace. Since they kicked out all of the residents, they only came back to bow down in the presence of the prince, and if they were lucky, the king. Madison cracked her knuckles, walking into the palace.

"No guards, huh. Well, I guess they've got the security where the mask is. Let's take a shortcut," she thought, then placed her hands on the ground. Madison blasted a hole into the ground, dropping below into the room. There was a small pillar with a black box on it. Just by the opening of the hole, wind mixed with strong pressure of dark energy was released, pushing Madison into the air.

"What the heck? It's like it's expelling years of energy! How old is that thing?" Madison asked. To her disbelief, it seemed like her voice was enough to get it to stop. The energy was still radiating off of it, just giving the air of truly dangerous. In the spaceship, the prince was introducing himself to everyone there.

"My name is Jett, and I am the makeshift ruler of the Darklands, the Prince. You may be asking, what is the reason for this absurd armor? Simply, I control the power of shadows. My body has to be under complete darkness for it to be effective." He explained, the most intrigued being Ms. Martinez.

"That makes more sense now. The reason the energies are all scattered across the world is because people can give off a very small amount of light, so it has to be rendered minimum, right?" She asked a question, and he nodded. "And plus, the day and night cycle is likely more common now, so it's better safe than sorry."

"Then you aren't going to enjoy Earthland. The only time you'd be of use is during the night time." Walter told him, gaining a punch on the arm from the demon princess.

"You can't just say that to him! He barely knows us!" Allie said to Walter.

"He's on the same boat as the rest of us. All of us have a weakness, some known and others not. It's fine for him to have one, because it means he's welcome to the team." He countered.

"It's kind of weird by not cutting us down, since we're branded as wanted criminals here. Especially me." James told the prince. Once his presence was known, Jett finally realized who he was.

"You're the previous prince, correct? The king said you were captured by foul beasts from Earthland!" He put together the pieces shortly after.

"If the old man said I was captured, then he's wrong. I was sent to Earthland on a mission, 'completed' it, then came back." James elaborated on his situation, to the surprise of Jett.

"...I see. If that liar ever steps foot on Darklands grounds again, I'll cut him down. He must've gone after you to try and bring you back, that filthy traitor." He began to walk out, but was stopped by Allie grabbing his arm. Since he went to the right, they were right next to the part with no windows, and the door had already closed.

"You can come with us to find him! Join us, and we'll stop him together!" She tried to get him to stay. Jett looked back to her, an unreadable expression on his face.

"I deeply apologize, Earthland girl. But, I must now attend to my people, and bring them back together. May fate collide our paths again someday." Jett told her, leaving the spaceship, but not before kneeling on the ground. The prince took the hand that was already on him, and in a show of affection, kissed the princess' hand. "Farewell."

She blushed, watching him walk further into the forest. "...What a nice guy."

....

"Wait, come on guys, have you not figured out who the king is?" Ash asked everyone, gaining their attention. Even the Darklands born must've forgotten, including James.

"Explain." Kim said, with the agreement of everyone else.

"It's Mr. Cook! How have none of you not noticed?" Ash told everyone. Once the topic was brought up, all of the dots were connected. He said he was from the Darklands, his power was mighty similar to Jett's, and James, unknowingly, referred to him as an old man by reflex. Now, he isn't exactly old, but he isn't young either.

"Ash, you're the best. When this is over, we're moving you to the Band House Extended." Ms. Martinez said to her. Before any reactions could ensue, a loud crash could be heard outside, prompting the Big 3 to go inspect it. In the crater was none other than the king himself, Mr. Cook.

"Oh, hello kids. What brings you he-" A swift figure bolted past the three, now standing behind the king. The figure was pure black, blending in with the sky. The wind was delayed, strong in its path. Once it reached the figure, it was revealed to be none other than the prince.

"I see fate has made our paths collide again. But, I assure you and your friends that you have no need to join this battle." A large gash on the back of the king appeared, dropping him down on his knees.

"You sure have gotten stronger. But not strong enough." The king said, the wound being healed by his darkness. He stood back up again, then snapped his fingers. Everyone surrounding him was teleported to the empty plain where the tower used to be.

"Still up to the same tricks, aren't you?" A voice well known to the Big 3 stated, descending down upon the fight that was going to ensue.

"Kim, go back to the ship! You'll be killed if you fight him!" Allie exclaimed to her, as her feet landed on the ground. Kim pointed two fingers at the king.

"Drop dead." A blast erupted out, pushing the other four out of the way using sheer force. Mr. Cook attempted at blocking it with his darkness wall, but it passed through like it wasn't even there. He stood there, as it passed through him as well. The blast deteriorated, leaving nothing but a smoke trail.

"I see, ex royal guard. You must've learned some new tricks in Earthland. Explains why it was so useless." The king laughed at her attempt. Kim just gave a peace sign.

"It's soul power. The cleansing may have not worked, but it called for some reinforcements." Kim said to him.

"The heck does that mea-" Walter almost questioned, but he got his question answered by five people surrounding them. Meanwhile, in the palace, Madison picked up the box.

"This isn't fun at all." It weighed a lot, but it wasn't heavy enough to stop her from carrying it. She began floating, flying out of the palace to the ship. As she got there, the box flew away from her.

"Are you serious?" Madison exclaimed, following it to try and catch it.

"Alright, are you guys ready?" Walter asked the rest of the Big 3.

"Yeah!" Allie answered, and James nodded.

"Let's g-" Before he could command the charge, the box flew towards him, knocking him over. Madison landed far away from them, out of breath from chasing it.

"Oops, sorry! You can continue with your fight!" The mask had emerged from the box. It was white, with a black dash across the middle, with holes where the eyes would be.

"You can't just pause a fight." James told Walter, as the mask attached to his face, releasing its dark energy on to

him. He summoned his shield, throwing it like a frisbee.
"Let's go!"

. . . .

Character Introduction: Madison

"Yo, it's Madison, section leader of the low reeds! I'm one of the bodyguards of the manager of Evil Remover." Madison explained.

"Doesn't the pay suck there?" Ms. Martinez asked her.

"Some questions are supposed to be left unanswered." Madison answered.

"Uh, okay. Go on."

"I'm gonna be the number one hero to prove everyone wrong! The ideal hero has to make everyone happy!"

Chapter 8

WHERE DARKNESS TAKES YOU

Kim stood on the sidelines, since her reinforcement tactic only helped fight the King. Soul powers are practically useless in the Darklands, only calling upon the strongest in the land.

"Mr. No Tengo, Gage, Ruby #1, and that other cool guy? What is this, a crossover episode?" Madison commentated, not wanting to interfere for the sake of watching how this battle unfolds.

"You foolish mortals shouldn't fight, for this is my battle and not yours!" Jett exclaimed to everyone surrounding him.

"All of us have something against him, so we might as well fight together!" James countered, setting his hands ablaze. He sent waves of fire towards Mr. Cook, who jumped in the air. Walter commanded his shield to return to him, and it almost landed a hit on the king.

"Allie, use your trident!" Walter told Allie, who summoned the weapon. She pointed it using both hands towards the king.

"I knew we shouldn't trust you!" She fired off a blast, which was very small and precise. Once it got even remotely close to Mr. Cook, it exploded. His darkness absorbed the energy, reverting it to nothing.

"Let's get him, Project Gotham!" Gage shouted, summoning his stand. His stand was surrounded by ZBoxes, each of them having one element assigned to it. Gage walked up to the king.

"Odd ability you have there." He stated. Project Gotham delivered a flurry of punches, none of them landing. It's like if anything tried to hit him, the king's body became intangible.

"What could we even hit him with?" Allie wondered. Jonny attempted to hit him with his power, which was a loud yell. Sure, it distracted him, but it didn't do much damage.

"Kids, I approve of your efforts. I wish I could fight you guys on equal footing, but it seems like I can't." Mr. Cook said to everyone around him.

"Wait a minute, the mask is on my face. Did that change anything?" Walter thought, then blasting the king. It sent him flying into a tree, catching him by surprise.

"Good call, Walter!" Allie told him, a verbal form of patting him on the back. The king teleported back to his original spot, with smoke coming off of him.

"Looks like the mask has claimed you, Lord of the Underworld. I shall bow down to y-" The king was uppercutted by Walter, sending him flying into the sky.

"Cut the crap." He took the mask off and stepped on it, releasing large amounts of energy. Kim's attack wore off, teleporting the ones summoned back to their hideouts, including herself, returning her back to the spaceship.

"Dang it! Come on, spirit. You can give me a hand during the Band Festival, right?" Kim asked Saxophone Salad, who was in turtle form.

"Sure. As long as your name is on the paper."

Down in the Underworld

Opposite to that of the Land Beyond, there's the Underworld. Usually named the Land Below. But, it's called the Underworld, because in some instances it can be accessed by the middle dimensions. The Land Beyond can't be accessed in any circumstance.

"Looks like you've found yourself here, true he-" EP Allie said to Madison, being punched across the face before she could finish.

"Shut it, scum." Madison then crossed her arms.

"Why are we down here?" James asked, looking at the multiple kinds of bones scattered around the area. The walls were made out of pure lava, and the floor was some red dirt like substance.

"The mask took us here, so we might as well explore." Walter answered him.

"This is literally hell." Allie stated.

"Not exactly, princess of the demons. Welcome to my world!" A voice said boldy behind them, floating proudly in the air. When they turned around to see who it was, all they saw was a floating skeleton.

"Interesting. You're the king of the underworld, I assume?" Jett questioned the skeleton.

"Yes, the name is Death! Wait, excuse me." The skeleton snapped, and a dark cloak appeared on them. A mask appeared over its face.

"I'm the oldest being alive, being billions of years

old, and everything. Even older than Xenos! Down in the Underworld, we get sent the worst of the worst. Once they land here, they can't get out, even by those crystals!" They explained.

"Really cool! I assume you've met the people who created me." Madison responded to him.

"Of course! If only they could see you now." Death sat down on the throne below him.

"How do you know that I'm the demon princess?" Allie asked them.

"Oh, the Oni royalty visit me a lot down here! Great company."

"Really? Can I meet them?"

"Sorry kid, but contact between the dead and the living isn't permitted. If I made the rules around here, then I'd let you."

"Then who does?" Walter questioned.

"The Greater Council, of course! I really shouldn't tell you guys about this, but I assume you'd keep a secret."

"She doesn't keep secrets." Madison pointed towards Allie.

"What?!"

"Let's see, how about I start with this! When powers were created 10,000 years ago, things were hectic. That's when the Demon-Human War began. So, the Greater Council sent 1 person down, and that's how the Sky Humans were made. The Greater Council makes deals with the governments of both worlds. They made all of the rules and regulations. All of the weird ways heroes have disappeared were the causes of the Greater Council." Death explained to the group.

"That's very interesting, Death. But, it's time for us to leave." Jett told the skeleton.

"Wait, how did you guys get here in the first place?"

Death asked them.

"There was this mask in the Darklands, so I took it, then it ran into Walter, and he wore it! Then he destroyed it." Madison quickly elaborated.

"You destroyed the mask? Truly remarkable! You must be my son!" Death praised, as a sword materialized in their hand. They sat up, and tossed it over to Walter.

"Is this the way out of here?" Walter asked, catching it. The sword was huge, as it was wrapped in bandages. The hilt and the guard were white, but the blade itself was black.

"Yup! Only my future successor could wield it, and I never thought I would see the day." Death began tearing up, somehow.

"How are you crying?" Madison asked.

"Oh, good point! I don't have eyes!" Death joked, the only person laughing being Madison, who referred to it as a 'skull joke.'

"How do I use it?" Walter questioned.

"Stab it in the ground, and it'll take you anywhere you want to go! Goodbye, so-" Before Death could finish, Walter teleported everyone back to the ship via his new sword.

"I must tend to my people. We'll meet again, won't we?" Jett asked the group, standing outside.

"Sure. We'll be back eventually." James told him, closing the door.

"Come on! I didn't get to say goodbye!" Allie complained, looking outside the window while the spaceship was rising.

"People are trying to enjoy their food." Madison countered, pouring a glass of water into a bowl while pretending to eat it with a fork.

"Yeah." Chloe said, doing the same thing.

"Everyone you bring in gets corrupted by your contagious weirdness." Ms. Martinez sighed, watching this encounter.

"Don't know what you're talking about. Anyway, we all know that we're going to forget this entire encounter, right? Mr. Cook still is able to sneak through our defenses and catch us by surprise." Madison told everyone in the center room.

"Who cares? I'll drop him again." Ms. Martinez responded.

"It isn't that simple. The government isn't in our favor, and he definitely bribed them into becoming the next number one hero." Chloe countered.

"I wouldn't say bribed. They're like minded. For all we know, he could've just walked up to them and made a silent deal!" Allie added in.

"We've got to remember this. If we don't deal with it before the Band Festival, he's gonna ruin it like that weirdo did." Madison said, upside down in the chair.

"Hopefully one of us will have a sparking memory."

....

Character Introduction: Walter

"Hey, it's Walter, section leader of the trumpets. I'm the makeshift leader of the Big 3, and owner of the Hero Corner Store. Before you ask questions, no, I'm not royal blood. I'm just a human." Walter explained.

"Alright. Now, what's your goal and your ideal hero?" Ms. Martinez asked him.

"My goal is to become number one like everyone else. The ideal hero has to be able to save everyone they can."

Chapter 9

RISING TENSION

Of course, like normal, they forgot the events that happened in the Darklands, but the ones who went to the Underworld didn't forget that event. Even Madison forgot what happened in the Darklands, probably pertaining to her ability to forget anything. Everyone who made it in DHB went, leaving the others there. Days went by, inching closer and closer to the Band Festival. The DHB kids returned, then a week after their departure came the Pre H.G.P.E concert.

"Oh, so we're playing in front of judges to see what we need to improve on?" Madison asked Kim. Madison was present for this last year, but just wanted to annoy her.

"Madison, I will backhand you to the next dimension if you don't shut up." Mandy told her, sitting right next to her.

"What was that?" The tenor questioned her.

"You heard me."

"I actually didn't, I wasn't paying attention." Madison countered. When they arrived, everything went by smoothly. They went through their pieces with the utmost energy. They were very much ready for the actual thing. After they finished, the bigger instruments had to be packed up and put on the trailer. Greeting and congratulating the accommodates was none other than the king himself.

He lowered the amount of power he gave off, to the point that it's noticeable, but not at all threatening. Once Allie made eye contact with him after pushing her tuba onto the trailer, she had a sudden flood of memories. Everytime she went to the Darklands, she remembered everything that happened. Including the meeting with the prince.

"Madison, it's time to fight!" Allie shouted over to her, as she was close to the bus.

"Really? That stinks. I wanted to eat a parfait. Who are we even fighting?" Madison yelled back.

"Ask questions later!" Allie teleported over to Madison, grabbing her arm. She then threw her at Mr. Cook, which definitely caught him by surprise.

"It looks like you've realized the truth. My bad." The king said to them, sliding back against the parking lot. The buses pulled off, leaving them there.

"Well, jokes on you, I have a super epic weapon!" Madison proudly claimed, reaching to find her canister. To her dismay, she didn't have pockets. Meaning it was somewhere in her tenor case.

"I can't just fight him on my own!" Allie exclaimed, as Madison ran back into the trailer.

"Yeah you can, you're the demon princess!" She acknowledged, fumbling around with the locks. Allie turned to face the king.

"Looks like your friend won't be able to help you. What a shame."

"Fighting you is going to be easy. If Ms. Martinez could beat you then, I can beat you now!" Allie charged towards the king, packing all of the punch she could in her first strike. All she did was run straight through him, missing completely. Right when she looked back, the king returned with a punch of his own, sending her flying. Allie caught herself before she could go too far.

"The weakness to his intangibility is to catch him by surprise, but he's extremely alert. This is going to be really hard." Allie thought to herself. Darkness began pouring out of the king.

"I don't want to do this, because it would be interesting to see what you would've turned into. Too bad, as it must come to an e-" He began, before being struck by the top of a stand. It retracted, revealing Madison with her 'super epic' weapon.

"Quit your monologuing! Using the super epic skills of a new power I learned, I shall defeat you!" Madison told him, while walking out of the trailer.

"A new power?" Allie asked her. Madison had also gotten her phone out of the case, and began texting on it behind her back.

"Yeah, it's really cool! Watch this!" She pretended to blast Mr. Cook. It did nothing at first, but then, Ms. Martinez appeared, punching the king with all she could.

"Sorry kids, but I'm gonna have to go again." Ms. Martinez told the 2, releasing energy so fierce it melted the king's darkness.

"Mom, you can't just leave us after the performance! What about the 7th graders? What about us? What about your family?" Allie constantly questioned.

"I will fight this alone. I don't need any help. I'm the adult here." Ms. Martinez answered her.

"Why don't you ever listen to me?" She shouted. The

hero turned her head, giving Allie a glare strong enough to cut through anything.

"I'm going! End of discussion!" Ms. Martinez marched towards Mr. Cook, the heat amping up everytime she took a step. She teleported him, then flying in the direction that she sent him. Anger built up inside Allie, as a tear rolled down her face.

"...She's gonna die, isn't she?" Allie asked Madison, who crossed her arms and looked away.

"There isn't any way to tell. But she's the number one hero! I'm sure she'll be fi-" She tried to be hopeful, but she was interrupted by Allie grabbing her by the saxophone harness and lifting her up.

"Madison, I'm being serious! You know what happens when she dies, right? Right?" She asked more frantically.

"Allie, I do know! Why can't you just believe in her winning? We still have Carowinds and everything! It isn't her time!" Madison released herself from her grasp, standing her ground.

"I can't believe in her because she won't believe in me!" They stood in silence while Madison searched for what to say.

"Breathe in and out with me, okay? I don't want you to explode in anger."

. . . .

In a far away wasteland, Ms. Martinez is fighting on par with the king, trading blows with him in the sky.

"Your will is strong, but ambition isn't traded for power!" King Cook yelled, trying to use his darkness. Ms. Martinez was releasing so much sun energy that it wouldn't come out, so she kicked him down to the ground. Once she saw him in the crater after the smoke cleared, she dropped down to the ground, charging a blast.

"Say goodbye." Ms. Martinez said to the king, about to blast him. Suddenly, her energy dropped immensely. She coughed up blood, dropping to the ground. Mr. Cook, now noticing that he had access to his darkness power, rose out of the crater, landing on the ground in front of the hero.

"Looks like you've lost your power, Martinez. If only your *master* was here to see you li-" The king was cut off by a sharp pain coming from his leg. When he looked down, he saw Ms. Martinez holding onto it with all she could. She released her superiority on him, the glow from her eyes being gold.

"Don't you dare talk down to him like that!" She poured all of her superiority onto him, completely removing the power from him. Mr. Cook got himself out of the grip, his power still gone.

"We must be on equal terms now, so I guess we can stop fighting!" He attempted to joke to escape the situation. Ms. Martinez slowly got back up, covering her mouth with her hand to stop the blood. She closed her eyes, focusing on the center of her energy. When she focused on it, the blood stopped.

"I don't care how long it takes. An hour, a day, a week, a month, a year, a decade, even a century, I'll defeat you!" Ms. Martinez called out, punching the king into the ground. Since she didn't solely train her legendary power, she still could fight without it.

"You're going to die. Don't you know legendary powers are tied directly to your life force?" The Darklands King asked, laughing, as he got up. Ms. Martinez noticed that the fire as her energy core was slowly dying out.

"I didn't know that. But, that makes me want to defeat you more!" Ms. Martinez attempted to power up to her ultimate form. It was worth a shot, seeing that it only worked in cases like this. The ground beneath her began shaking, rocks flying up. The energy appeared, almost blowing the king away, but he stood his ground. Instead of being a normal fire, the fire suddenly turned blue.

"Impossible! How can you do this?" Mr. Cook questioned her, stepping back slightly.

"By breaking my limits!" Ms. Martinez reeled a fist back, to deliver the final blow. When she tried to punch him, it was extremely close to his face, but the energy disappeared. Steam began pouring out of her.

"I win." The king chuckled, as Ms. Martinez passed out.

"Consider yourself under arrest." A voice unknown to him said behind him.

"What are you talking about?!"

In the Band House Extended

Everyone was settled in their rooms, knowing everything that went on from Madison.

"This is all my fault, so I have to get stronger." Madison told herself, sitting down in the chair that she had for her desk. She began thinking about the events that lead up to this.

"If it wasn't for my existence, none of this would be happening. I'm not even supposed to be alive....!" She thought, looking at her hands, then clutching them.

"No time for sulking, tenor! Pick your head up and go on!" She heard her door open, and from there was Allie. Man, she really talks to her a lot. Kind of convenient that she's right next door. "Yeah, what is it?"

"...I wanted to thank you for what you did earlier. So-"

"Who are you and what did you do with Allie?" She stood up, getting in a defensive position.

"It's the real me, dimwit! Don't I normally show gratitude?"

"No." She responded quickly.

"*Anyways*, I was trying to ask if you wanted to go somewhere. Like, on a-"

"A date?! You really are an imposter! The real Allie is smitten with the Prince of the Darklands, Jett!" Madison dropped the act, lowering her guard. "But really, just because I helped you? Is that it?"

"Don't think about it too much. I don't want to say anything you don't want to hear." Allie explained. Madison thought about places that would be open around this time.

"Let's get snow cones!"

· · · · · · · · · · · · · · · ·

Character Introduction: Allie

"It's Allie, here! I'm a part of the Big 3, and I work at Evil Remover! Before you ask, yes, I am just human. My goal is to become number one, and I don't need a reason for it! My ideal hero is me!" Allie finished in all one go.

"...Wow. Good job, I guess."

Chapter 10

BREAKING THE LOCKS

The tension in the air could be cut by a knife. No one knows what happened to Ms. Martinez. It's like the heroes went completely off the radar.

"We obviously can't go to school. We have to make sure the 7th graders don't go crazy." Chloe stated, sitting on the table.

"It's like we're babysitters. Man, I hate kids." Allie responded, dusting off the shelves. The low reed instruments were supposed to be there, but they got moved to the school once they started.

"Technically, we don't have to look after them. Kim could handle them just fine, right? I mean, she's the great leader of Evil Remover!" Madison joked, on the table along with Chloe.

"Well, none of us have actual jobs that we need to run." Mandy added, on the floor. Meanwhile, in the Band House, the 8th graders left there, accompanied with the rest of the Kelli Squad, were the actual babysitters.

"With this mighty oboe, we shall rule Earthland!" One of the 7th graders exclaimed, standing on a bunch of chairs.

"Yeah!" The rest of the 7th graders plus Kandi and Kim agreed.

"Why do we have to be here again?" Alex asked Ash, who was sitting next to him.

"Beats me." Back in the Band House Extended, Walter used his sword to open a portal.

"I'm going to train in the Darklands. Who's coming?" He questioned everyone downstairs, putting his sword over his shoulder.

"Me!" Allie immediately answered.

"I said train, not flirt. Madison, you want to go?"

"Sure. You going to the Underworld to train with your dad?" Madison got up and walked towards the portal.

"Yup."

"Alright then! I'll be even stronger than you guys when I get back." She said in pride, then ran into the portal. When Walter followed suit, he closed the portal to open another one. He walked into it, returning to the Land Below. Madison jumped through trees, going to a familiar base. Once she saw it, she made a huge leap towards it, completely overshooting the shot and landing in the ground.

"Madison, what're you doing back here?" Maddie asked, opening the window. Madison picked herself up, then dusting her pants.

"I'm only here to train! Teach me your ways!"

"Oh really? You must've run out of masters in Earthland." Madison nodded excitedly.

"Yeah. Mary taught me how to use Drive Two, and I was gonna get Ms. Martinez to teach me Drive Four, but she's…" Her expression dimmed through each word. She couldn't finish the sentence.

"I see. I can teach you- Wait, don't cry!" Unknown to her, Madison had dropped a few tears, and her eyes were full of them.

"I'm not crying, what're you talking about?" More tears came down, as she fell to her knees.

"Alright, I've decided on your first training regimen. Be prepared for my emotion training!"

Through three days of training, Madison came to terms with her emotions. This, in turn, opened up a new view of her Drives. Previously, she could only access 5% of Drive Three, and even though it isn't mastered, she now has full control over it. She fully realized that her Drives were portrayed by emotions. Drive Two was Fear, Drive Three was Sadness, and her new drive…

Was rage. Negative Drive brought out her worst emotion, so she learned to control it, to be named Drive Four.

. . . .

Madison began powering up, her aura changing from blue to purple, then mixing with black.

"Let it all out! Everything you're mad at!" Each thought increased her aura, darkening the color more. It kept on increasing, to the point where she almost overexerted herself. Before she could, Madison absorbed all of the energy, making her dizzy.

"Are you sure this is working? I'm tired." Madison complained, almost falling to the ground. She stood up those entire three days, not sleeping at all. You had to watch your back in the Darklands.

"Yeah, you've got it under control. When you get back to Earthland, you have to find out what happened to Ms. Martinez. That's when you'll be at ease." Maddie told her. Suddenly, the sky went from black to blue, returning to how it is during the

yearly tournament.

"Rather odd. It's been like this since the beginning of time." The Darklands Prince said, watching as the cursed instruments fell to the ground. The souls in the instruments, after many years, were finally put to peace.

"My eyes!" Madison shouted, not having seen sunlight in three days.

"You're definitely not used to this, are you?"

....

"The Darklands is saved now!" Madison exclaimed, now in the Band House Extended.

"What'd you do?" James asked her.

"Oh, nothing. It's just that the instruments are lying around everywhere." She sat down on the floor.

"It means the curse was lifted. That means she's alive somewhere!" Chloe stated.

"We need to go find her, then. Let's go, one person instruments." Madison tiredly cheered, then got up. Chloe helped her out the door, Kendall following close behind.

"So, where exactly do we look? They went off of the radar." Kendall questioned Chloe, who put Madison on her back. She was still awake, just not kicked into gear.

"We can look underground. There's a few villain bases that can hide presences." They began the search, the air waking up Madison a bit more.

"Alright! Let's go!" Even with the obvious bags under her eyes, she still looked forward to this with pride.

With renewed courage.

They searched far and wide, finding various villain bases. Most of them didn't have any life in them, except for the last one. It was the abandoned base of U.V.C, Chloe's home as a villian. When they walked in the entrance, Chloe dramatically smelt the air.

"Ah yes, so nostalgic. I remember every single person I killed in he-" She began, cut off by Madison.

"We are not here to think about dying. We're trying to find Ms. Martinez." Kendall lifted up some of the stone rubble.

"This has been here for a year or two. Looks like bandits or villain rejects decided not to come here." He tried to sense any energy, but then again, it was extremely hard. The presence was masked.

"Section Leader, can't you access some sort of secret area?" Madison asked, sparking a memory.

"Of course! All you have to do is…" Chloe walked towards the middle of the base, the floor where Madison met Serena. She blasted a hole in the center, which had a hallway under it.

"Blow up this part!" She motioned for Madison and Kendall to follow her as she jumped in. When they all got down there, they realized that it was just an empty space.

"Do you remember the code?" Madison whispered to Chloe, who nodded.

"Electricity." She said, and another hole opened below them. Kendall looked down, and back at Madison.

"…Crap." They both said, as they all began falling down. Once they reached the ground, Chloe looked around. Sure enough, the heroes were there.

"Ms. Martinez, you've got explaining to do." Chloe told the hero, who was just notified of their presence.

"Uh…explaining?"

Chapter 11

CONSEQUENCE

Every action brings the inevitable consequence. There's always the bad side. Usually it's subtle, if it's with a good heart. This event was big though. Huge. The government tried to cover it up, but the people were quick to notice. Ms. Martinez was the only hero with such an amount of fame to be allowed such a pedigree. The rest of the heroes, Señora Salcedo and below, weren't noticed. Sure, in the community they were in, yeah, pretty popular. But the outside world only knew about The Martinez.

With her disappearing, it was noticeable. It sent the world into turmoil. Had the government been lying to them this entire time? What else have they been lying about?

Then, there's of course the villains who were defeated by her previously. They've come back to power, gaining more attraction and members. Ms. Martinez wanted peace, and now it's the complete opposite.

There's also another issue. H.G.P.E is in a few days. If

they want to have their best performance yet, they're going to have to deal with this the hard way. Up until this point, the only time they've left their state was to go to the City of Gold. They were going to leave for Carowinds.

"Again, I deeply apologize for causing this. Maybe if I was more careful, this wouldn't have happened." Ms. Martinez told everyone, having them all gathered into the Original Band House.

"This isn't your fault, Ms. Martinez. In fact, it isn't any of our faults. We need to think strategically here." Ms. Stevens comforted her. Madison stood up.

"We can't just leave. If we do, our success at the concert would be at risk, as well as the house itself." Madison said, also trying to think of the best way they could go with this.

"I'll deal with them. I technically started all of this, right?" Chloe asked Madison.

"We *need* our Bari, Section Leader! You can't leave!" She responded.

"Speaking of Baris, I know exactly who we need." Allie said.

"...Why would we need the instrument?"

"Not the instrument, you idiot! We could get Brandon to go and deal with them." Mandy got up.

"I'll deal with them also." Without waiting for any objection, she left.

"That problem is dealt with, then. But, there's another issue." Chloe began.

"What else?" Madison asked.

"The Band Festival."

....

"There's more heroes out there. We just don't know about

them." Madison sighed, after explaining the situation to Ms. Martinez.

"So we don't know how strong they are. They probably aren't able to deal with the villains." Chloe continued for her.

"This is a real bad situation you've got us in." Ms. Stevens told Ms. Martinez.

"I understand that! Dang it. How're we going to do the Band Festival now?" She asked, bringing it back to light. It was completely forgotten about by everyone. The number one hero had forgotten about it herself. She was too caught up with her job to remember.

"Either we postpone it or deal with the situation." Señora Salcedo said.

"We'll just have to decide that later. Everyone will surely be happy when they find out Ms. Martinez is alive." Madison remarked.

"Was that supposed to be sarcastic?"

....

Mandy was flying around using her flames, looking for villain bases. The easiest route was to just blow them up, and fight them if they wanted to. Most villains were just kids who wanted to join in on the trend, so I guess they could be referred to as juveniles instead. None of the villain bases she came across were a threat, so that was fine.

While taking quick glances around, she ended up bumping into something, not paying attention to whatever was in front of her.

"Ow! The hel-" The voice began, before noticing Mandy.

"Brandon, get out of my way!" She shouted.

"No, you get out of *my way!*" He countered, getting face to face with her. They then both sighed, turning around.

"Let's just split up. I'll take half." They said at the same time, blasting off in opposite directions. For once, they are in agreement.

Meanwhile, in the abandoned city of the Future, a certain someone stumbled upon a wormhole.

"Ah yes, in this twisted future, the Darklands and Epitomus remains."

Chapter 12

STATE OF AFFAIRS IN THE KINGDOM

You thought this was going to be about an update on Prince Jett and his kingdom, now that the king is gone. You're partially correct. This is the Darklands, yes, but the Future Darklands. Instead of being another dimension, the Future is a similar reality to that of ours.

Here's the difference. Timelines are in the same year, but things are different. Other dimensions can be in other realities, and the sky's the limit in possibilities of what they could be. Realities are different from each other, and have their own timeline and dimensions.

In our Madison's reality, the only dimensions are Earthland, Darklands, and Epitomus. They aren't the main timeline, far from it, but could be considered so. Actually, considering the majority of other timelines have ended because of the Darklands events, this is now the longest running without any slip ups. All of that timeline stuff was from that mysterious voice, so take it with a grain of salt.

So yes, they are now back on track, technically, as Timeline A.

Now, back in the Kingdom. Future Madison had failed to kill the majority of people in Earthland at the time, though she's convinced she did. Most of the Earthland people escaped to the Darklands. It's been about seven years since then, and the Darklands has changed. The King never went mad, so there aren't any instruments floating around.

It's brighter outside. A better place than Earthland now. Technology is slowly being embraced, to the point of automobiles.

"There's a wormhole open in the Mysterious Forest. Think you can handle any intruders?" King Cook asked the guard near his royal chair.

"Of course I got this! I'll be back!" They excitedly said, running off. Once they got outside, they jumped far. Far enough to land exactly where they needed to be. The certain someone had just gotten out of the portal, and made eye contact with the guard.

"You must be the royal guard." EP Allie said to the guard, who drew their weapon, which was a clarinet.

"The hero of the Darklands, Kim, in the flesh. What business does a foreigner have with us?" EP Allie began to charge a blast, but it was cut off by hand cuffs being put on her.

"Ah, a tyrant I see. You'll fit in well with the Underground." Within a few minutes, EP Allie was locked behind bars. The bars weren't normal iron. Being near it disables your powers, and makes you weaker. Future Kim was now walking through town, making sure the people were okay.

"How's work so far?" A voice coming from behind asked her. When she turned around, it was another guard.

"You know, arresting villains. It's nothing, though. What about you, Elizabeth?"

"Patrolling the town is fun, too! You want to join me, or do you have to go back to the palace?" Kim thought about it for a bit. She was sure that the king could handle himself if trouble would arise.

"I'll come along!"

Back in Earthland

They were finally at the final villain base, and got rid of it with ease. They were now across the country.

"Now the people are safe." Brandon muttered, as the ice evaporated off of his hand into steam. He had frozen the entire building.

"I guess working with you is a good idea after all." Mandy told him, while standing behind him. Brandon just barely glanced over his shoulder.

"You still use your flames as a villain. Get over yourself already." He began to walk off, but was stopped by Mandy grabbing his wrist.

"How about you get over yourself! Just because your house burned down years ago doesn't mean you can blame me for it!" This flipped a switch in his brain, making him slap her hand away.

"And just because your family rejected you years ago doesn't mean you can blame me for it!" He countered.

"Everything is your fault!" They both shouted at each other.

"All you do is boast about how strong you are! You lost against me!" They continued saying the same things about each other. Their frustrations were the same. Their level of hatred against one another was the same.

"I've got a Band Festival to do." Mandy shot off, abruptly leaving Brandon there after their argument. The mention of his house crossed the line on his field.

"Always running away ...when will you grow up!" He exclaimed, continuing on his path on missions. Mandy was using her flame blasts in anger to get there faster.

"I need to knock some sense into him when this is all over."

....

"Walter of the Land Below, son of Death himself, would you like to go somewhere with me?" Allie asked the fellow Big 3 member. This was surprising. Wasn't she messing with the other prince earlier?

"...Moving on fast, huh. Sure Jett would love to hear this." He responded. They had just finished another boring mission, and were waiting on him to fix his motorcycle. It suffered a big crash in Bronzeland, and still wasn't working well enough for him. "Didn't he like, kiss you on the hand?"

"H-How did you know about that?"

"You told me when you called me the other day?"

"Oh, I forgot about that! Well, just forget about it! Let's have fun!" She cursed herself inwardly for slipping up and mentioning that. He finished up by giving it more gas, and hopped on.

"There's a nice restaurant downtown. It's kinda pricey, but I also heard that it had a hero license discou-" Allie got on the seat right behind him.

"You don't have to tell me twice!"

In the Band House Extended

"Alright, Band Festival is accounted for. This time, we definitely won't be interrupted. I'll personally make sure of it." Ms. Martinez thought, while organizing her papers in her office. Meanwhile, upstairs, Madison had a reed in her mouth.

"Power skips generations randomly. Powers had been skipped for two years straight, but they aren't counted in the statistics. I can't say I was born without powers, because I was never technically born," she thought, her mouth piece standing upright on her desk right next to her. She was throwing her ligature in the air to waste time, seeming as if she had nothing else to think about. All of her pieces were mainly easy, due to her not having hard parts. Madison didn't need to train either. Power wasn't exactly the main thing of her problems.

"A quest for happiness? Who needs it when the world is at stake? If anything, having a broken spirit chain is a benefit. The reason why I have it, no clue. Having to worry about any person is a waste of time." She mumbled, grabbing her mouth piece so she could put everything together.

"The number one tenor doesn't need anyone!" She claimed, putting her mouth piece on the desk. She sat down in her chair and got out her music. It's time to do some studying before HGPE. The Band Festival was about a week before her birthday, which meant it was sure to be great. Truely an exciting day.

In the room down below, Chloe was training. She needed to practice swinging around her sword. She had to perfect it so she wouldn't lose.

"Even if there's a Bari stronger than me, I still am on top of the world now," she thought, slashing the air. Chloe never had swordsman training, so maybe meeting a sword master would benefit her. She only had a few days, but her potential

could bring her far. She sighed, her sword vanishing into the air of the small room she was in.

"I think it's time for a master." Outside, James was dodging bullets from Kim's new weapon. It was a sniping type of weapon, with a scope that had night vision. She was on the roof, firing shots down at the past prince. Kim had to get definite permission from the ex-prince that she was allowed to shoot at him, so she could get over her fears. Back under the ocean, in the Single Town office, Mary was dead asleep on Madison's desk, as Junior shook his head.

"Now what do I do with this," he thought, holding up a weird note that was left outside the office. The paper had some sort of ancient scripture, which turned into a necklace. It had a tenor on it, a very small replica that is.

"Lawbreaker! Out of my office!" Mary awoke her power in her sleep, throwing vases at Junior. He screamed, running out while dodging the objects. When the door was shut, the throwing stopped.

In an unknown desert

A wagon traveled through the sand. There was nothing pushing this wagon to get it to move, but only one thing was heard. A harmonica. Inside of the wagon was a long black case placed vertically, accompanied by a number of cases, each different in sizes. There were 7 of these cases in total, the rest of them laid on the bottom planks. On top of it was a figure, the source of the harmonica. A western town was in the distance, and once they spotted it, the music abruptly stopped.

"This is the worst part of the job." Once they reached the saloon, they opened the door to the inside of the wagon and dropped the instruments outside, except for the one not placed carelessly. They closed the door, and got back on the wagon, as it began rolling away as fast as it could, before the door to the saloon was opened. Two figures burst through the doors, almost breaking it in the process.

"You were three days late! We needed those three days ago!" One of them shouted, as the other sighed.

"Sorry, the repair shop was robbed by bandits, and I had to get them myself! You should be grateful that I got them!" The figure on the wagon yelled back. The wagon disappeared into the sunset. The one who sighed sat down on the biggest case, putting their hat down.

"Bailey, I'm pretty sure you're overreacting." They said.

"I get the instruments are hard to move, but three days! The repair shop was robbed two days ago!" Bailey complained.

"At least Tag went and got them." She stopped her tirade.

"Yeah, Chloe. You're right."

Chapter 13

WILD WOODWIND WEST

You Let's continue the journey into this western town.

This is the dimension of gunslingers and fights. The death count has a higher rate than Earthland.

"...And that's when I said, that's not my tenor, that's my-" Madison was cut off by Bailey and Chloe almost breaking the door. Without hesitation, she pointed a gun towards the entrance. When she realized it was just them, she sighed, putting her gun back in her holster.

"It would've been a way funnier joke if you finished." Allie replied, as Madison sat back down.

"Insult me one more time and you won't hear any jokes." She attempted to threaten Allie, which was practically thrown out the window.

"That's unless you can't hear anything first." One of the middle sized cases was thrown at Madison, who caught it by the handle. The sudden weight dragged her arm down. This was her beloved instrument, Saxophone Saturn. It was... of age, but she could still play it.

Aside from the random destruction of doors, the saloon was filled. Madison always hung out around it, so she snagged a seat before the waves of people came in.

All of these people have one goal. To be the number one gunslinger. The fastest hand in the west. The keenest eye. The instrument was an *identification* of sorts. To fit them in different categories. Some instruments were grouped in with others for simplicity's sake. There were leaders of these groups. They were the best gunslingers. After the saloon emptied out, the day was over.

Not for the saxophones.

"Ten pushups, now!" Elliot, one of their section leaders exclaimed, as the altos proceeded to count off their pushups. The low reeds were scattered around the surrounding area. Madison pointed her gun towards a target that was set up dozens of meters away. She fired it, getting close to the middle.

"Darn it." Madison mumbled, tossing her gun into the air to flip it. Right when it was caught, she shot the target again. She almost made it again.

"I'm Tag," he began. "So that means I'm the best gunslinger here."

"Then why aren't you section leader?" Chloe asked him.

"Cause I don't want to do it."

"On the ground!" Madison for some reason had her tenor out, and pointed it towards Chloe.

"On my knees?" Madison blinked.

"No, on the ground!" Chloe did as told.

"Is there a bandit or something?" She asked. Madison put her tenor back in her case and wiped a tear from her eye.

"No, just wanted to see if you listened to me. You di-" Before she could finish, she yelled, getting her gun out of her holster and immediately shooting a figure from far away. Bailey looked at the altos, still doing their routine, and shrugged, putting her hat back on.

"Bet it's those tenor bandits. They take tenors in, switch them out with wooden planks, and leave a note with '10'000 dollars for it back'." Tag said, going to investigate.

"They probably don't make any money. Oh well, come on, N2." Madison told Chloe, following the taller Bari.

When appointed to your section, you're given a number. This number can change, depending on who graduates. Sometimes the section card could get mixed up, and end up in a different section.

Madison's number was X1, not knowing where the X in saxophone was until she thought hard enough. Her card was printed last. It seemed to be in alphabetical order, but if that's the case, why X?

"Windy? You're the tenor bandit?" Madison exclaimed, still pointing her gun directly at the culprit.

"Uh...Yes?" Chloe took out her gun as well.

"We don't show mercy on tenor takers." She added.

"I have a proposition!" Madison lowered her gun to listen.

"That would be...?"

"If I bring back all of the tenors, can I join up with you guys?"

"Bring us back the tenors, and we won't fire." Tag countered the offer. With her hands up, Windy backed up, now standing.

"I'll be back eventually." She jazz ran off, leaving the saxophones there.

"Tag doesn't need help getting instruments back." He said, putting his gun away.

"If she doesn't show up in three days, we'll go and raid them." Madison stated.

Three days passed. A gunshot could be heard outside of a seemingly abandoned building.

"Low reeds are out here! Bring the tenors right now!" Madison jumped out of the back of the wagon. There were seven tenors scattered about, circling the building. Each of the cases were in their own, separate conditions.

"Uh..how about we conduct a search?" Chloe questioned.

"Tag says there ain't any instruments there." Tag added, opening up the first case. A horrible stench could be smelt, the demon that it was now released.

"Oh brother, that instrument stinks!" X1 exclaimed. There were other instruments that smelled bad, obviously not being opened in years. There was one rather shiny one, but it was broken. The rest of them were broken without question. Except for one.

The low B flat and B keys weren't on the front of the bell, but were on the back side. It had stars on its bell design. The octave key had a 50% chance of working.

"This weird tenor needs a name." Chloe offered.

"Remind me why you name your instruments again?" Bailey asked them, confused about their reasoning.

"Because Tag said so." Tag replied.

"Let's call it Saxophone Sketchy!" Madison proclaimed, lifting it off the ground.

"What about the other tenors?" Chloe mentioned.

"...Leave them."

On Earthland

Madison woke up in a cold sweat, clutching her bedsheets as

hard as she could. When she realized she was in her room, she sighed, touching her head.

When she realized that she was still in a dream, she gulped. The tenor looked down at her body, and noticed that she had on her hero outfit this time, without the cape. It was the same black jacket that covered up the long sleeved black shirt. Her pants of the same color covered up her bandages underneath pretty well, and the part metal boots were there as well, even the gloves.

"That's weird…" Madison got up and left her room, roaming the halls of the band room. "I have a feeling I need to leave…" The air had a red tint to it, she noted. She could hear how bustling the Band House Extended was normally, but never saw any people around her. The halls were darker than usual. If this were night time, it would be completely dark unless someone turned on the lights again.

The loudest noise she could hear over anything was the sounds of her shoes hitting the ground.

"Maybe when I see my teacher again, she'll be happy to see me. I can't seem to remember the last time I saw her, but I wish I could again." A voice rang throughout her head, stopping her walking. Madison looked around. It echoed for a few seconds after.

"Who was that?" Shaking her head, she continued on, choosing the stairs would be the best route.

"If I could've stayed just a bit longer, I could've gotten to know my dad better. Living with him would be crazy, am I right?" A different voice laughed. Madison took long steps down the stairs to the floor below hers, now having to walk down that hallway.

"I want to be seen as a great warrior across this land! All of the recognition I could dream of!" An additional one.

"Sometimes I wish my reputation did a 180 so I wouldn't drive fear in people's hearts. I kind of like it sometimes, but I

think it would be for the best." Madison went down another pair of stairs.

"*It feels like all of the battle damage I have is just weighing me down. If I could fight him without that worry...*" Another hallway.

"*The position I had in my path was gone in a day. Maybe I could reclaim that title as King.*" More stairs.

"*If I woke up and had a family, I don't know what I'd do. But I'd definitely be happy, since I never grew up with one like everyone else.*" That voice in particular sounded familiar. Has she heard that before?

"*I want to reclaim my place as the leader. If I left before I could do it, then they should all be brought back!*" Right when she thought it was getting repetitive, she finally reached the bottom floor.

"*Everything I make is just for you guys. If everyone recognized what I could do, I'll finally be realized as a great inventor!*" When she got closer to the exit, a voice that was louder than the others began talking.

"Where are you going?"

"To my home." Madison answered.

"Home? Isn't this where you belong?" They questioned. She stayed silent. "...I see. So, you still haven't accepted. We'll meet again soon, then." The double doors opened on cue for her. When she walked out, everything faded to white.

Chapter 14

THE LIE

"...and then the tenor said, 'All Saxophones are equal!'" Madison exclaimed, clapping her hands together, closing the book she was reading.

"But you're a computer!" Chloe responded.

"But nothing! The Tenor Adventures themselves said that we're all equal!"

"I don't have any powers." Kim bleakly countered.

"Equal!"

"Ugh, just shut up already! We don't have time to yell before the Band Festival! Put your uniform on!" Allie shouted at Madison, who still had on the pajamas she slept in.

"Okay, okay. Stop shouting and I will!"

In the Band Festival Stadium

The air was different from what it was the previous year. Since

Ms. Martinez and the band have been a popular subject since the City of Gold incident, it was going to be a lot more lively.

It's the first time in years that heroes have been accepted into the general public.

The rate of people joining a hero program has been rapidly declining for a while. The rate of people getting a pro license is even lower than that. Even if there's a decline in rates, that doesn't necessarily mean that there aren't a good amount of heroes left.

When it comes to professional heroes, it is a small amount. Only really the top ones are left. But, those are the ones that have the experience.

There's still the high schoolers.

Ms. Martinez leaned over the edge on the top part of the balcony, looking down into the stadium. She sighed.

"Someone apart from us is a traitor," she thought. In one of the rooms, Madison laid upside down in one of the chairs.

"Hm, am I *really* not human?" She pondered. The door was ever so slightly opened, and then slammed open. It was Kim. Madison's eyes went down from the ceiling to make eye contact with her.

"The Darklands King and the high school band director are two different people!" Madison's eyes narrowed.

"Wait a minute," she began. "You're telling me that there are two Mr. Cook's?" Kim nodded frantically. Madison sat upright in her chair.

"Plus, he's been here for a while now! I don't know how we didn't find out."

"Well, then there's probably someone that's been messing with our memories!" Madison crossed her legs and arms. There was silence for a few moments.

"...crap." They both said.

Meanwhile, in one of the hallways.

"Ms. Martinez, are you sure it's fine for us to come here? Exams are coming up, and it's really busy..." A voice spoke over the phone.

"Think of it as a well deserved break. You can do some scouting too! They'll be all around the campus, so most of them probably won't mind you talking to them." She responded, reassuring them.

"Well, if you think it's fine, I'll tell the others." After sharing their goodbyes, the call ended. In the hall of the opposite side of the stadium, Madison was walking throughout the entire building, thinking of possible traitors.

"So far, none of them have really shown any signs. It has to be someone that's close to Momendez, and at the same time someone who's been here awhile." Madison stopped in her tracks.

"One of the Big 3, maybe? They're the only ones that could've been wiping them from the start. But why...?" Around the corner came the sound of someone bursting into a fit of laughter. Madison quit zoning out and peaked around, trying to see who it was. It was two people she hadn't met before, but it felt like they had.

A distant memory Madison couldn't pick back up.

"Be quiet, Rose! They don't need to know that we're here!" The other one said in a hushed whisper. That one. She had definitely seen her before. But where?

"Sorry, it's because of Joe." Rose responded, serious for a second. The other figure was visibly confused.

"...Who's Joe?" Rose held back as best as she could.

"Joe Mama!" She answered, bursting out in laughter. Madison looked closer, trying to recognize their outfits. It was like she knew where they came from, but she just didn't remember.

The person sighed.

"Rose, that joke wasn't funny awhile ago and it still

isn't now."

"It's just that you keep falling for it, Julia!" That name. Madison remembered it. It seemed like the memory was suppressed. Maybe she had met them before.

It's time she fixed the lie.

Madison emerged from the corner she was observing from, catching the attention of the both of them.

"See, I *told* you that you were too loud."

"You can complain when you can beat me in a fight."

"Excuse me?"

"Uh," she began, stopping their bickering that seemed like it would go on for hours. "Look, we don't know each other, but can we talk? I don't know if you're here for the festival or not, but there's a few hours left before I have to report somewhere."

They agreed.

Madison uncovered the truth of everything up to this point. She now has knowledge of everything that she forgot about. Plus more knowledge to add on top of that.

She has also formed a bond. Rose and Julia have both made a lasting impression on Madison in the hours she had with them.

Through them, she may have put a pin down on her true identity. Something she's been questioning as early as she can remember. The memories that were probably altered.

Flashback Begins

"The power wheel theory isn't real. Or, at least partly." Julia explained, to Madison's surprise.

"Then how was I powerless?" She questioned.

"You were never powerless. There was no number

one hero before Mr. Shine. He only became number one because it was weird without one. In his fight against 'Cook'," she continued, adding quotation marks. "It was soon revealed that there was another version of Cook. The one in Earthland is a completely different person. The Darklands Cook was from Epitomus. You're also not Prototype Zero or whatever it's called. A lot of things have…changed behind the scenes."

"So you're telling me that I inherited my powers from my parents, the curse wasn't a curse, there's two Mr. Cook's, and…" At this point, Madison's head was spinning. "You think she's a traitor?!" Rose nodded.

"Julia has been researching the Darklands thing for the past year, and since the memory wiping has affected us too, she looked into that."

"Now that I think about it, I do remember seeing something in my vision when I was on the moon…"

"It's the gold block, right? Couldn't you read it in person?" Julia asked her.

"I could, kind of, but it was like someone had changed it before we got there."

"Through the research, I conclude that 'the one' is…!"

Chapter 15

COMPARED TO THE COMPETITION...

"We can't win this." Madison sulked, now back in the waiting room she knew no one was going to be in. "They work for the king himself, so if we aren't careful…"

"Hey, quit being sad over there and come on. The 1st event is going to start soon!" Chloe peeked into the door. Hearing her voice was enough to at least get her up. Her mood? A little. Her actual body? Yeah.

The Band Festival was more lively than the last time. Given that there were more people participating, the final round was set to be more intense. Well, if they even got to that round. There was a long time traitor walking about. You could even add an s to it, given some other suspicions she had.

Who knows, maybe those people that talked to Madison were liars. She had just met them, anyway. But something about them let her know that they were not joking around. She felt a sense of familiarity. The Power-no, Zero user knew exactly who that person was, so when the dots were connected together by two people that seemed like they knew what they were talking about, it was heartbreaking.

She should've figured this out at the start.

To be fair, the person (people?) had been changing memories around, getting rid and adding stuff together for it to make sense. Maybe they made a slip up one day?

While walking behind Chloe, Madison went through anything that sounded sketchy with the current memories she had.

....

You know, they could've made a stupid mistake. Well, if there was never a number one hero, which meant I never had a master, then why did we have to go to that one tropical island?

Speaking of that island, Black Forest, I can remember an unknown person mentioning my past family. According to Mandy, one of them said they didn't know who the heroes were, and had never heard of the rumor that the number one hero died there. That was something that raised suspicions to her.

Then, there was the girl who talked to me both in the Black Forest and the Room of Mind and Truth. She looks exactly like Julia. Maybe the truth she was trying to tell me about was what the world really is? She kept on referring to herself as we, so maybe that included Rose as well?

Now that I am thinking about this, I also remember those 345 prophecies. So, if everything those two told her were true, those scriptures didn't refer to me. I was just mindlessly listening to those prophecies and thinking that they applied to me this whole entire time. So, what really was significant to my existence? That Xenos stuff was probably true, and maybe the 'Prototype Zero' stuff as well-

....

Madison broke out of her train of thought as she walked straight into a wall. While she was massaging her head in pain from the inconvenience, Chloe put her hand on her shoulder, worried.

"Hey, you sure you're okay?" The tenor nodded, putting up her signature smile, without what was usually behind it.

"Yup! All good! It's all fine!" Chloe hesitated a bit, before dropping pursuing this any further. It was probably all fine like she said. They continued on their walk together.

....

So all that soul chain mumbo jumbo was just some weird thing my mind made up, or was it something those guys put in my head to make me remember that I had it at some point? Power World also reminds me of a weird dream. But wait, who did that 345 thing actually apply to? I can see the Drives still being a part of me, and maybe those lines I can activate are from my own power too, but that means the prophecies applied to someone else!

Her eyes widened, as she came upon this revelation. Without her knowledge, the bari had a close eye on her. Chloe's concerns increased, since she couldn't guess on what she was thinking about.

The question is who? There are so many times they could've helped us by using that extra strength, and they decided not to? Huh, they might as well be feigning innocence this whole time. That suspect list that Julia gave me was spot on. Those people definitely could've been conspiring behind our backs. Since I know who the traitor is, thanks to her and Rose, this'll be way easier to track down. They'd have to talk to each other frequently though, and no one on the list talked to them that often.

Then again, I couldn't see some of the people as suspects. Julia told me she was being extremely cautious, and put anyone that we recently got in contact with on the list. Such as some of the Darklands and the City of Gold folks. It was funny when Rose laughed at the list being extremely long, and when they began bickering, but how she knows about the Darklands events is far beyond me.

And then there's the situation where there's two Mr. Cook's, and how we've been completely disregarding the other heroes as if they didn't exist. I mean, I've always been a big hero fan, but all the merchandise I can find is of Ms. Martinez and the top heroes. Maybe they tampered with that as well...

I'm pretty sure that those heroes are mad strong. It seemed like Julia and Rose were a part of them, and the power I sensed from them, although masked, was incredible. Still, you can only get so strong as junior high kids, and they're high schoolers. At least, I think so. They never confirmed their age to me, but they looked that way.

I guess I'll have to make a decision pretty soon.

. . . .

Madison stretched a bit, proud at the conclusion she had come to. Even though what she had to decide would be sure to affect some things, turn them to worse, she had to do this.

Thinking about this somehow took a big weight off of my shoulders, and kinda cleared my head.

"...Hey, bro?" Madison asked Chloe, as they stood at the exit that led to where the first event would be held.

Relieved that she finally spoke up, as the unordinary silence from her was scary, she sighed, then glanced at her.

"What is it?"

"Before we head out, I need to fill you in on something. Promise you won't spill it?"

"Of course!"

A few minutes later

"...Woah." Chloe simply stated. Madison had just explained to her the entire jist of the situation. The tenor nervously laughed.

"Heh, yeah. We have to be extremely careful," Going based on a hunch, she turned to the door behind her. "Isn't that right, Mandy and William?" The former fell from the wall on the opposite side of the door, and the latter stepped over her.

"While she just gave us away, yes. Your secret is safe with me." The oboe got up and dusted herself off, kind of embarrassed from the entry she made in front of her past superior.

"You know what? An ex villain, a burnt stick, a minimum wage worker, and a copy machine. This team isn't half bad. "

Chapter 16

CONTEST

"The first event is a battle of strength! Without using your powers, hit the machine as hard as you can!" A flat area outside of the stadium was used for this event. The trees were further back, which meant that all of them stood in a half circle around the five machines. There wasn't necessarily an order to how they got there, so it was first come first serve. This was just about as broadcasted as normal, with drones that had cameras flying around. The loud speakers were just as loud as normal despite the echo in the stadium, which meant the narration might be a tad distracting.

"Ugh, you're way too loud! Turn down that megaphone!" Allie complained in annoyance to her own mother, her hands covering her ears.

"Fine. I just won't use it." Ms. Martinez semi-grumply turned it off, placing it on the ground. "Anyway, here's how it works! On this board here," Behind her, a huge screen on the side of the main building turned on. "A ranking system will appear based on how much you score! It can be anywhere from 1-1000. From there on, the Top 50 will advance to the next event!"

"So it's 200 to 50, huh? Way to eliminate dead weights." Mandy commented, getting a light tap on her shoulder from her previous leader.

"Hey, quit it. You're going to scare the children." Chloe scolded her.

"So, who wants to go first?" Their teacher questioned them. Everyone looked around, not wanting to be the first in case they scored low. Moving through the crowd, a figure suddenly came forward. It was Kim, standing proudly.

"I'll go! I need to set an example!" She said, stretching. Madison shed a tear.

"Wow, she's so incredible."

"Don't you dare say that ever again." Allie told her.

"Whatever, princess."

"The first contender, Kim from the clarinet section! Set the stage for how intense this festival will be!" She walked closer to the machine directly in front of her. The main camera in the arena broadcasted a close up on Kim's smug face.

"Never thought she would go first. Did you?" Julia asked her partner in crime (Hero Crime? What?!) Rose.

"No, I didn't. Let's see how high she scores." Since powers weren't allowed in this test of strength, Kim had this easy. She reeled back her right arm.

In the history of the Band Festival, whenever the Strength Competition was selected, the highest score in base strength was 925 set by The Martinez herself. The closest to that was set by a hero by the moniker of Tag, which was 872.

And with a hard hit and a jumble of numbers by the machine and on the big screen, at the top of the leaderboard, Kim had a score of...

1.   Kim - 122

Though short, the business owner received applause for the first time in a while. She smiled, walking back to the crowd.

"I did my job." James wordlessly strode past her, also hitting one of the machines as hard as he could. He almost busted the machine with the amount of force he put in.

1.   James - 626
2.   Kim - 122

He went back, leaving a distraught look on the other clarinet's face. "Man, what the heck!" She thought to herself. Her jaw dropped even farther when her rank was slowly but surely going down.

In a matter of minutes, the rankings had turned on its head.

1.   James - 626
2.   Walter - 612
3.   Chloe - 499
4.   Amy - 487
5.   Mandy - 426
6.   Chimera - 407
7.   Bailey - 381
8.   Kelli - 350
9.   Aaliyah - 270
10.   Kim - 122

....

"Ah, so close. Good job." Walter went and high fived

his fellow member of the Big 3.

"Hey, send me the rankings when everything's over. I have to do something real quick." Mandy told Madison, who nodded.

"Sure."

"But now, it's my turn." Allie smirked. This time, she would use all of the strength she had, disregarding the whole demon identity crisis. This was 100 percent all her. This time, the one she punched exploded, but the calculations were still sent in...

1.   Allie - 704
2.   James - 626
3.   Walter - 612

....

"Do I really have to go?" William asked, not interested in a strength game. He had other things he wanted to do, like start that one series he found.

"Just go so we can get it over with. There's a break after this anyway." Chimera told him.

"I'll go at the same time, so we can be even." Sid offered. He thought about it for a second.

"...You owe me." Instead of punching the machine like everyone else did, he kicked it.

4.   William - 543
5.   Chloe - 499
6.   Amy - 487
7.   Sid - 444
8.   Mandy - 426

....

A hero watched on from the audience in the stadium.

"Those were saxophones, right Matt?" The figure questioned the one to his right.

"Didn't they announce that when they were going to the machines? You need to pay more attention, Vic." Matt told him.

"Their scores are really good. I just wanted to make sure…"

"Last we have from the Low Reed Section, Madison!" The tenor in question stared down the machine.

"I can't use a single drop of power, huh? Fine by me." She stated, grinning. She went last because she didn't want to bother the rush of people trying to get in the top 50.

Madison pulled back. "Smack cam!" She shouted in her head, not wanting to make a fool of herself.

1. Allie - 704
2. Madison - 682
3. James - 626
4. Walter - 612
5. William - 543

And soon, the scores would be finalized. Kim went from Number 1 to Number 47 in just under 30 minutes. Well, at least she barely made it in. Knowing her luck, she'd barely scrape by and make it into the final round. The break was starting, so, knowing that they wouldn't have much time, our new group of the ones who knew the truth met up.

Madison was a bit shaken up while sitting in her chair, fidgeting a bit more than usual.

"Hey, what's up?" Chloe questioned her. They were in a room rather isolated from the rest, to avoid any unwanted ears listening in on them.

"It was weird looking at the leaderboard. When I

heard that Aaliyah, of all people, scored higher than Kim, I was shocked. I still am." William put down his book.

"That also raised a few alarm bells to me. But we have to be cautious of everyone at this point. Even *Elizabeth* scored higher than Kim." He told her.

"If we're pinning blame on everyone in the Kelli Squad, then what about *Kandi*? Even she scored in the Top 20." Mandy had her arms crossed.

"But what's really on my mind is that one of the Big 3 is a huge suspect. Sure, I can hit harder than two of them, but their powers are another story. They all have *control* over something." Madison held up three fingers. "Time Control, Elemental Control, and Mind Control. To top it off, Walter has the power of the Underworld, and Allie is half freakin' demon. The fact James can keep up with them is impressive in its own right."

"So we can't even trust them, huh?" Chloe asked, and they all looked disappointed.

"We could take a gamble." Mandy brought up to them. Hand now holding up her cheek while propped up on a table, Madison's interest had gone up.

"How, exactly? You want us to get one of them to join us?"

"If all of them are on that list that Julia mentioned, then we'll just have to ask her who's the least likely to be it." William added on, catching on to the oboe's drift quickly.

"Section Leader! You know what to do." Madison commanded, gaining a salute from the bari.

"Yousoro!" Chloe teleported out of the room, and a few seconds later, arrived back with the mysterious hero that Madison had met earlier. They all stared at her intensely.

"...D-Do you guys have a question?"

....

Julia was more than happy to explain to them that specific part of her research. She had been studying it for a while, after all.

According to her, the least likely suspect in the Big 3 would be James. Despite his Darklands origins, which initially landed him on the list, since he didn't agree with the evil King Cook's wishes, this placed him at the bottom of that. Since she had to study other things about everyone involved, Julia also told them that if need be, Prince Jett could also be of help.

After telling William she'd be happy lending him her notes when this was all over, Julia said her goodbyes and returned back to where Chloe picked her up.

"This is great." Madison smirked, proud of the decision they'd come to. As they'd have to leave early for the next event, they stood up.

"Let's head out."

Chapter 17

AN IMPORTANT ANNOUNCEMENT?

"Now, it's time for the second event! Since we have to lower the amount of people for the main event, it's time we begin the most favorite game mode, The Coliseum!" Ms. Martinez announced, the applause ringing throughout the stadium. Indeed, The Coliseum was extremely popular for as long as the Band Festival was going, even if there weren't many people around watching it back then.

Everyone who passed the Strength Contest stood in the arena, awaiting the explanation.

"There are 50 contestants, and the lowest points you could have is 10, if you're 50th. The number one spot is worth 500 points," The big screen showed a picture of Allie taken from her destroying the machine. "Second is 490," It then put up Madison grinning when she was cracking her knuckles. "And so on. Everytime you ring someone out, the points they collected are frozen and they can't get back in the arena to fight. The points they're worth are added to your own, and whoever is in the top 20 gets to advance to the final event."

"For example, if Kim, who's worth 30 points," Ms. Martinez pointed at the clarinet. "Ringed out Allie, who's worth 500-"

"No, never in a million years!" She interrupted.

"Kim would be worth 530 points. So keep on ringing out people to boost your points!"

With one hand on her hip and the other up to her chin, the tenor was pondering this in her head.

"So basically, if I keep knocking 7th graders out of the ring, then moving onto the weaker 8ths, I'll be number one in no time," Madison thought, planning this out in her head. There was no doubt that a like minded individual had the same plan as her, so she'd just have to move faster than them. Since she has more control over her emotions, her Drives would be more efficient as well.

"Is Kandi back yet?" Aaliyah whispered to Bailey.

"She just got here. Being late isn't necessarily far from her reach…"

"Where did Walter go?" Allie asked James.

"He went on a quick shopping trip. Something about a gift."

"Here are the rules. You can't use any weapons, and you can't actively try to harm someone on purpose. That will land you disqualified. Please, don't try to destroy the arena. We used the best material, and that cost a lot. Also, try not to fly all the time…"

The alto William had just explained to James the plan that they had, including the main suspect he was told of. The clarinet was a bit skeptical at first, but when William went on, it made more sense. Of course there wasn't a risk with anyone overhearing, as they were all paying attention to the Festival.

"So that's it."

"...Wow."

"I know..." They were not people of many words.

"Alright. 3...2...1..." Madison eyed down everyone she was going to knock out in order. She lowered herself closer to the ground, that superiority glow coming from her eyes. "Go!" Madison bolted off, activating Drive Two. Instead of punching people, she settled on using her shoulder to her advantage, shoving people out of the ring. With her landing back on solid ground, the steam flowing off of her, her points had been boosted.

She had avoided Kim, going for everyone else in the 40-50 range of status, and knocking all of them out. Including the business owner, that would be 550 points, excluding her 520.

"And in only 15 seconds, Madison has taken the top spot for 1010 points!" Ms. Martinez exclaimed. Said tenor bent backwards as far as she could, as an incoming Mandy and Chloe went over her and knocked out their fair share as well. A big fight broke out, with Madison as everyone's center target.

"Excuse me, but I'll be taking those points of yours!" Sid tapped her shoulder, which meant he copied some of her powers. He's seen how Madison's fought, so he knew how it worked. Though, the muscle memory of her power ups weren't included. Sid tried to blast her, but she backflipped out of the way, right where William was. They were back to back, since he was focusing on fighting off Aaliyah, Elizabeth, and Kelli.

"Power Blaster!" He fired off numerous of the blue energy waves at Madison. Her and William turned around at the same time, effectively reversing their position. The alto copied his section leader, countering all of his blasts to the exacts. James jumped into the mix, him already having his share of knockouts.

1. Madison - 1010
2. Walter - 830
3. James - 770
4. Allie - 500
5. William - 460

Walter had taken 110,120, and 130 points, while James took 140, 150, and 160. Soon, Chloe took 170, 180, 190, and Mandy took 200 and 210. Chloe and Kendall were teaming up on Bailey, knocking her out, though Kendall got the final hit, getting him 400.

1. Madison - 1010
2. Chloe - 990
3. Walter - 830
4. Mandy - 810
5. James - 770
6. Kendall - 760

"Don't you think it's weird that this is going on for longer than usual?" Mandy brought up to them, trying to outrun Walter, the one who controls time of all things, in a speed battle.

"Now that you mention it, yeah, it is." Suddenly, Allie bust threw the huge fight, catching the Kelli Squad (without Walter) off guard, knocking them out. Aaliyah was 300, Elizabeth was 310, Kandi was 320, and Kelli was 390.

1. Allie - 1320
2. Madison - 1010

3.   Chloe - 990

Walter froze Allie in place, prompting James to send a gust of wind in her direction. As soon as she was unfroze so she could be knocked out of the ring, she guarded, taking it head on. Mandy grabbed Kendall and threw him at her from across the arena. He turned into his Phoenix form and tried to headbutt her.

"So you're all going against me, huh?" Allie commented, effortlessly dodging Kendall.

"You are a threat, you know. Knocking out four people at once isn't exactly something we shouldn't be worrying about." Madison replied. James sent a barrage of lightning bolts directly at Chloe, who blocked it by making a barrier with her rainbows.

Meanwhile, in the booth at the highest point of the stadium where Ms. Martinez was overseeing the battle, Ms. Stevens came in.

"We have a problem at the Band House, and it's urgent!" She exclaimed, surprising Ms. Martinez. Just in case, she turned off all of her microphones from the room.

"What's going on over there?"

"You have to see it for yourself! Hurry!"

Sid was eliminated by Walter, gaining him 430 points. He caught him by surprise by countering a move that wasn't from him, and instead from Chimera. Her punches hit so hard that when she hit Walter, he almost got knocked out as well. Allie, distracted by Mandy and Kendall, was almost taken out by Kim. Using her Mind Control, she made Amy fight the poor clarinet.

Kim jumped and dodged, doing anything to get out of her explosions. Copying Madison's actions, Kim just so barely managed to knock her out of the ring, and even she knocked out a few people...

1. Allie - 1320
2. Kim - 1020
3. Madison - 1010
4. Chloe - 990
5. Walter - 890
6. William - 830
7. Mandy - 810
8. James - 770
9. Kendall - 760
10. Chimera - 610

But, before they could continue on, Ms. Martinez landed directly in the center of the arena, stopping all of them from their fighting.

"I really hate to be interrupting this event, but it's been postponed!"

....

"Why did you postpone the fight?!" Allie yelled, seemingly furious about it. They were in the biggest meeting room on the campus.

"Because the Band Houses were burned to the ground! All of our stuff was scattered outside!" Everyone had a shift in tone. The princess who was angry before switched to shock.

"So they just tossed our stuff outside? What...?" Madison asked, taken aback by this information. It was very odd for them to do that.

"We need to go there now!" Mandy shouted, running out of the room. Everyone followed her out a few seconds after.

...Who did it? Who burned their homes down to the ground? And why...?

Chapter 18

IN A TURN OF EVENTS...

"...This can't be a prank or anything. But why would someone do this?" Madison questioned, watching both houses burn to the ground. They had already fallen over, missing all of the stuff that the perpetrator took out.

"It's got to be Brandon. I swear, I'll go kill him..." Mandy clenched her fists, beginning to walk off. Chloe stopped her, stepping in front of her.

"You of all people should know that he doesn't want anything to do with fire. He probably doesn't even remember where the Band Houses are!"

"Then who did it? Tell me, since you know everything!" She demanded. William broke their fight up by getting in between the two of them.

"There's only seven people here with abilities related to starting fires. Judging by how they moved all of our stuff out beforehand, it'd have to be someone who had the time to do so. If the Band Houses had nothing wrong with it before we left," He began, analyzing the situation. "It's someone who left in the middle of the festival. Does that sound familiar to anyone?"

Everyone looked around at each other as the fire began to subside.

"What if it was just an attack from some hero hater or something like that? That isn't exactly uncommon." Allie spoke up.

"What if they were one of us?" James asked her.

"That's a great question, James." Walter added on.

"Plus, why in the world would they throw our stuff out? Shouldn't they just burn it all?" Kendall also asked.

"A person with fire related powers who left in the middle of the festival and doesn't have a liking for heroes. With all of our stuff on the ground, they should have a good scope of where everything is. Right, Mandy?" Madison asked her friend, as if pinning the blame on her. All attention was put on her.

"Yeah, it sounds a lot like *her*," she responded vaguely.

"Look, our home just got burned down. Can you hurry on and tell us who it is?" Ms. Martinez told Mandy.

"All evidence points to it being the Kelli Squad Member and part Flute Traveler, Kandi." Gasps and shocked expressions spread throughout the large group.

"What?! There's no way I did it! I can't even create a fire that big!" She defended herself.

"Why would it even be her? She's weak!" Allie joined in.

"And that's what she wants us to believe." Mandy said.

"You haven't even talked to her once, and you expect us to think that you know about anything she's done?" Chloe questioned the Big 3 member.

"Maybe you're one too, princess." Madison added, smirking. With their execution of the question, there's no way that she could lie her way out of it.

"...Come on, guys. You already *know* I wouldn't do something like that! Right, guys?" She looked at Walter and James, who both remained silent. Their expressions said 'We don't want anything to do with this.'

"And I thought that you were my daughter. What a turn of events." Ms. Martinez stated, sighing.

"So what do you have to say for yourselves?" Kim asked them. As they were effectively backed into a corner.

"Taking our memories, changing them for your benefit, even going as far to burn down our home. You know, we should just take you out right now." Mandy prepared a fire in her hand. Suddenly, a small ship-like vessel appeared above the two, landing behind them. From the top of the vehicle came out the Darklands King himself.

"I see that you've finally found out the truth. Yes, these two have been working for me from the start. While Kandi did take some...*convincing*...she did join us in the end." He began talking. Ms. Martinez backed up, not wanting to fight him right now.

"What do you want from us?!" She shouted to him.

"On the contrary to your belief, I've come here with a proposition. With all of the memories we've gathered over the years, not just from you people, but the entire world, it's time for my *special ability* to come to fruition." The King explained to them. "Not just an ability, but the *Ideal ability*! I believe that this will be in the best interest of all of you. You wouldn't want it to be over."

"Thanks for telling us beforehand, old man. Why don't you leave already?" James told him. King Cook looked at the previous prince.

"I gave you a chance to join my Kingdom for the rest of your days, but it seems like they've already gotten to your head. No matter, this will be all over in a day's time."

"What do you mean?" Walter asked him, arms crossed.

"I believe our time is up."

"Before we go, let me say a few things." Allie stepped up to the platform he was standing on.

"Of course." He answered, going to the inside of the ship. In a dramatic switch of facial expression, the facade she held up for all of those years had finally left.

The truth has been revealed.

"I hope some of you come to your senses and join us in the utopia that's about to be created. As you should know now thanks to the efforts of the ever so powerful hero who had everything handed to them, I've been tricking you for a few of the past years." She said, directing that particular comment to Madison, who crossed her arms and smirked.

"You know, your work was really obvious and sloppy. I could read that golden scripture." She explained how she found out. This was partly true, since she found out by getting that vision of the real readings, and the message from Julia and Rose. It was a matter of connecting the dots once the exact words had been deciphered.

"I hope you know that who I sided with isn't the only thing I've been hiding. I've also been masking my p-"

"Power, yeah. We already know this. You 'hated' your demon side that you discovered, which meant you only used 50% of your full potential. But using the demon energy even while you despised it was suspicious. Surely you'd prefer to just control people like you've been doing, right, Demon Princess of the Oni Royalty?" William had also been able to put this together, after being interested in the topic.

Even if she never met the Demon Race herself, she

initially found out about them from meeting King Cook while he was disguised in Earthland. Allie became obsessed with the *idea* that she *could've* had an entire army; no, entire race under her finger. She began hating the human race for fighting against them, and willingly messed with their memories for the King's benefit.

All for something she would have never had.

"I hope you know that there's no chance that we wouldn't have noticed you asking us all the same question." Walter stated.

"'If you wanted one thing to happen, what would it be?'" Ms. Martinez added. Now that they all know for certain that she's the traitor, everything that just wasn't right to them had been coming together. They didn't believe it at first, and chalked it up to overthinking.

"Your plan was horrible." James simplified.

"You heard them. So, what's the final word? Your declaration to kill us?" Madison questioned her. Allie remained silent, furious at this.

The ship started rising into the air.

"Wait!" Ms. Martinez began running over to the ship, but it disappeared before she could get there. The sky was still as bright as ever, and only smoke came off from the remains of the houses. Mandy held some of the ashes in her hand.

"...We'll just have to go home."

•••••••••••

It was dark. Late at night. Everyone else in the City of Gold had already fallen asleep. Though, one resident was awake. *Very* awake.

Loud sounds of crashing and clattering could be heard from outside of the Single Town office. Mary had been out doing some minor jobs when she got a call from the president, saying she needed to come down to do some work. When she picked them up with Junior's taxi, she expected her to have a somewhat cheerful energy like how they usually did. It was quite the opposite. The older girl didn't even attempt to make conversation because she was afraid of making things worse. Yes, even the 'world's strongest' was afraid. So that's how she found herself standing guard outside of the office.

The whole place was in disarray as Madison threw countless items to the walls, shattering them into pieces. She tried not to lash out, she really did. But…Allie was her closest friend. Bonds like those were hard to find or replace. When Madison picked up a picture frame, her hands shook as she contemplated whether or not this was worth it. Several tears fell onto the glass, the final layer protecting the picture of two friends together. It took thinking back to the burning buildings for her hesitation to fade away. With a loud crack, she shattered the thing into pieces with her bare hands.

Mary had to fight back shedding a tear herself as she heard the faint distraught cries of her superior, amidst all the other chaos going on. All of a sudden, it all came to an end. It took minutes of an uncomfortable silence until her president opened the front door, walking down the stairs.

"So…what now, president?" She asked. From where Madison was standing, she couldn't tell what she looked like. There were a few glass shards stuck in her hands, but nothing punctured far enough to draw blood.

"…Take me home. I was gonna go to Couple Town, but I don't think I can handle it." Mary tried to offer her friend a comforting gaze when she finally turned her head to see her.

"When you get home, take time to rest. You need it. We can both forget this ever happened."

....

This was the first time that Madison stepped foot in her own house in a while. Throwing all of her stuff on the ground, she sighed.

"At least we managed to catch them red handed in their lie. Who knows what else they've been hiding from us? Especially Allie..." she thought, laying down on the couch. She turned on the TV in front of her, the last channel she had watched being the one the Band Festival was usually broadcasted on.

"The Festival Events have been canceled due to the homes that the participants lived in being destroyed by a fire. We will try to refund all of your tickets." Ms. Martinez said on the screen. *While they were disappointed, they were mostly understanding.*

Madison went to her room and switched to more comfortable clothes, scrolling through her phone while on the bed. While she was still upset that they burned down the houses, she was grateful that they decided to move their stuff out beforehand.

"This was the wildest day I've had in forever. Well, aside from that one time I got a hole in my stomach and almost bled to death..."

....

"I'm home!" Ms. Martinez exclaimed, walking into her house.

"Oh wait, I don't have a daughter anymore," she thought. That was until she found Mandy and Chloe in the building.

"We don't have a house," they explained. Well, that was true.

"Welcome, I guess. Wait, how did you get in...?"

. . . .

"Back to the office like normal." Kim sat in her chair, looking at her paperwork. There wouldn't be any reports this late at night, so she closed up Evil Remover.

"...I think I'll go to sleep somewhere in Single Town. I'll call the taxi at the shore." All of her stuff in her backpack and in another bag, she left the building. The Flute Travelers probably went to the City of Gold also, so she wasn't going to be alone in this.

. . . .

The Kelli Squad Hideout was left intact, which meant the only one who had to move in was Walter, who chose to just go to the Hero Store. Along with Kendall, Bailey, Ash, William, Sid, and Chimera. There were many rooms to spare in case something like that happened, and also a basement for Kendall to put his stuff in.

"Yeah, this is where we live." Elizabeth explained to them.

"Not a half bad place." Walter commented.

"We have to base our operations somewhere, you know." Aaliyah told him.

"I know that already."

. . . .

The Hero Store had a room in the back where there was a couch for breaks and stuff. James slept on the couch while Walter closed the store.

"I wonder what he was talking about," he thought, then walked back to the room.

．．．．．．．．．．．．．

Madison woke up in the garden again, waiting for the voice to talk to her again.

"The King has activated his ability." The voice finally said to Madison.

Do you know anything about it?

"It's something that changes the entire world depending on what memories they take."

Chapter 19

THE WORLD

Madison woke up, stretching both her arms and legs. Her first instinct was to look at the news on her phone.

Breaking News: Evil Removal Owner Saves City of Gold!

"*Woah! Kim must've done some awesome stuff. She doesn't have any powers though, so that's very limited...*" she thought. She scrolled down, trying to find more information.

The business owner saved the One's Above from an organized attack that was planned behind the scenes. They were taken out with minimal effort before they could even get inside the bubble.

"...Can she even breathe underwater?"

It was done using the inventions of a criminal turned good. His most notable invention being a mechanical dragon, he's created many great things for the good of the planet.

"Huh, I kind of can remember seeing a metal dragon thing." Madison put her phone in her pocket, and got out of the bed. She opened the door, and went down the stairs, looking around her kitchen. The tenor heard rummaging from behind the counter. "...Hello?" She cautiously asked. Arose from behind the sink while holding two metal spoons in each hand was...

"Uh, do you know where the bowls are?" They questioned her. Madison couldn't recognize them.

"Wait, who're you?"

"Who am I...? Are you still asleep?" They began. "I just got back from my business trip, and you're going to pretend you don't know me? Wow, some kids these days."

"I mean, a lot's happened these past few years. I almost died, I got kidnapped, I almost died..."

"K-Kidnapped?! Who kidnapped you? No one should be taking my *child*," they exclaimed.

"You're my mom?" Madison was freaked out by one, a stranger showing up in her house asking for bowls, and one, them being her mom. When did she have one?

"Yes, I am. Well, first, cause you're probably concerned about the spoons, my friend is still out on the town training with her student, and she's going to be here soon. I wanted to make something to celebrate!" Her mom explained to her. "But how did you forget about me? Did you not remember the family photo?" Madison blinked, now sitting down on a chair at the counter.

"Family...photo?" Her mother handed her the photo in question. It was in a wooden case, the glass protecting it. It didn't seem to have any damage, so it looked sort of new.

"This is from when you got accepted into that band program of yours all those years ago. I was so proud of you." Now that she looked at the photo closer, her mom did look kind of familiar. From somewhere...recent?

"Who's the person to the right of you?"

"Oh, that's my coworker, -----. Come on, you remember her! We taught you how to use your power!" That name...

"Right. What was your power again? I think I forgot it." She laughed off her question.

"I'm the 5th Power user, and you're my kid, so you're... Super Powerful! Get it?" Madison thought she was the 5th Power User. It seems like questionable puns run through the family.

"Yeah." She chuckled, handing her mom back the photo. "When exactly did you get back from that project thing?"

"Yesterday morning. When I came home, you weren't here yet, so I went somewhere else." The day before. Madison feels like she's been forgetting something very important.

"I think I was with my friends. It was some sort of contest." Contest. What kind of contest was it?

Madison felt glass break, and through the door came presumably the student she was talking about before. William's her student?

"Can I talk to Madison outside real quick?"

"Sure, you can."

....

"I'm assuming you've broken out of this lie, right?" William asked her.

"Lie? What's going on?" Madison responded, not understanding what was going on.

"The new building in the center of the city, and with that, the revival of the demon army. The sudden revival of people who were dead. People suddenly gain positions of power. I've seen it all." He stated. "The world itself has been put under a spell. In turn for that spell, an evil king rules over us." Eyes widening, Madison stepped back.

"Slow down! You mean the demons are back and in the city? Why Cappy City of all places?" She exclaimed quietly, not wanting her mom to hear.

"Who knows. I have my own personal idea on who's sitting on that throne right now, but that doesn't matter. We have to go and see where everyone is."

....

They went throughout the presumed locations of everyone's whereabouts. First on the list was the closest to the house, Evil Removal. This could possibly knock out a few from the checklist, but surprisingly, it was taken down.

"...I *would've* guessed that they ran out of business, but no, if the place isn't here, then Kim's in Single Town." Madison sighed. Calling the Junior Taxi would be kind of risky, so they'd have to check that later down the line.

"And it's way too dangerous to go any further into the city, so let's go to the Darklands." William replied, smoothing out some of the wrinkles on his coat.

"How in the world are we supposed to get there? Do we even know where a teleporter is?" He took out a key and stuck it in an invisible lock. When he turned it, a portal around the same size as them opened. "Woah! You can do that?!"

"Quiet down. We're in the middle of the city."

"If you clearly look around, people are paying attention to their own lives, which have changed for the better. They don't care!"

"...Anyway, yes I can do that. All high ranking personnel can do this at any given time."

"Noted. Let's go!"

....

In the Darklands, where the light has returned for good, things were looking different. Cities were booming across the place, instead of it being deserted ruins. The Negative Kingdom in particular had been restored to its lively self. Where there was nothing but cursed instruments going around, the palace was filled with actual people on the inside.

"This...clothing...is rather uncomfortable. I believe I prefer my armor." Prince Jett told the new king in front of him. His metal armor had been replaced with the Darklands Royal garb. It was black and dark purple, and extremely similar to James's older outfit. The only difference was his sword on his hip.

And speaking of James, he was the new king. He had on King Cook's previous outfit, fitted to his much smaller frame. The crown was on the desk in front of him.

"You'll get used to it. I made sure that your power can still work, even with the really bright sky. I hate it too..." Over the prince's shoulders was a long cape that could go over the rest of his body, but he didn't want to use it either way. It was really hard for him to walk around town without his armor. Since he was used to the heavy weight on him, Jett was thrown off of balance while walking, and he almost tripped in front of the townspeople.

"Why do *I* have to get married off to an Earthland girl? Is that not against Darklands law?" He questioned the other young king, who shrugged.

"The last time I checked, that's not one of the laws."

"The 30 Darklands laws. That one was number 30..." Jett took out the old scroll it was written on, and sure enough, it wasn't there, as if it was erased...

"There are only 29 laws in the Negative Kingdom,

and it's been that way for years." The prince was perplexed by this. He remembered memorizing all of the laws, and there were 30 of them. Something was already fishy about this.

A knock came from the door, breaking him out of his stupor.

"Come in." He assumed it was one of the servants or guard checking on them, but no, it was the son of Death himself. Instead of the bare minimum of casual that he wore on the daily, he wore a black short sleeved dress shirt accompanied with dress pants of the same color. The sword he got from his 'father' was compressed into a tiny knife that fit into his belt.

"Hello, Walter. How's it going?" James walked up to him to greet him at the door.

"Everything's going fine, I guess. My dad makes me run errands all the time in the world of the living, and I stopped by here to say hi to you guys." Walter explained to them. The three of them went further into conversation, without knowledge of two listening in on them from outside.

"Hear that, William? We've got an arranged marriage on our hands." Madison said, looking at them with binoculars. William rolled his eyes.

"He doesn't seem to want to be involved with whoever the 'Earthland girl' is, especially if he can't remember her name." He responded. The tenor paused, remembering 'Earthland girl' from somewhere. She's heard him say that previously, and who that was referring to was at the tip of her tongue.

"Hey, do you remember anything from before now? I have a weird feeling that I'm forgetting a huge chunk of something…" She asked. He thought about it as well.

"All I know is that a bunch of stuff changed, and that wasn't the same as before. Come on, let's get moving."

....

"Oh, you know, kids will be kids. They'll be back by dinner time." Madison's mom told her friend that showed up at her house a few minutes after the two left.

"Well, since they're gone, and we have the time, what do you say to having a sparring session?" She replied.

"I made food, and you just came from training! Aren't you the least bit fatigued?"

"It's just that we haven't had the chance to since everything started all those years ago! Please…!" She begged.

"Ugh, fine. Just don't do anything stupid."

....

The Number One Hero, The Martinez, had retired from her position, due to her power being gone. In her place came Señora Salcedo, and another addition as well…

"Can you please come to the training for the interns today?" A voice said to her from outside of her door.

"Why do I have to do it? Can't you get Stevens or something?" Ms. Martinez countered, already busy with training another intern at the same time as the other ones.

"She's busy taking a group to space! Don't you remember that that was normal now?" That's right. Ms. Stevens had normalized space travel recently, so she was taking people there left and right, returning when she needed to. That left the previous hero rather lonely.

"…Yeah! I'll go, Shine!" She told the Underground Hero, Number Zero. Mr. Shine left from the door, going back to where he came from. "Hey, are you fine with training with the older kids?" Ms. Martinez quieted her voice down to turn her attention towards her personal intern.

"I don't mind." Chloe responded. After a large sum of heroic deeds, her mentor decided to give the bari her license early. Her reputation did a 180, since she was previously the strongest of a villain organization.

"Alright then. Let's go there later."

"...And as you can see there, the revival of the dead." William told Madison, who nodded. They were passing by the area, looking at him in particular.

"How weird."

"Hey, get out of my way! I was going in that direction!" A familiar voice yelled from above.

"No, I was! Quit following me everywhere I go!" A less familiar, although memorable voice interjected. When the two looked up to the sky, they noticed that Mandy and Brandon were in the town, presumably chasing after the same thing.

"...There's just so many wrong things here." Madison deadpanned. Brandon doesn't even go to the same school that they do, or live in the same area, so him being in town is a rarity.

"I would've been more surprised if they weren't fighting." William noticed that the scars that the two of them had on their faces when he first met them were gone, but decided not to bring it up. The one thing he remembered them for was when he saw a small bit of their fight in the Darklands.

"Okay. I think it's time we go and pay a visit to that palace."

Chapter 20

THE KING, QUEEN, AND JACK

'*Even if that one dream may have come true, there could've been another one that was held closer to you. They will make any one, or few, dreams come true, if it didn't go against the King's will. They will do anything to appease the King's desires, even if it has losses on their end. If worldwide happiness is what it takes to stop people from challenging him, then it will be so.*'

That is the Ideal Reality.

Where one ruler above all grants the wants of the masses, where they cannot be opposed, and if that were to happen, they have two loyal underlings to do his bidding. The Queen, and The Jack. Those two have wishes that are only second to him, which will grant them even more power as a single unit.

The Queen has summoned a powerful ally to join their forces from another land, the Joker. By inviting them into their domain, swaying them if they have to by any means necessary, they will gain another ally.

The Jack, by one of their wishes, has a bodyguard replicating that of which they obsessed over the most, the Ace. The twisted liking to that of their protector at all costs was stronger than the one to the ruler themselves.

"Ah, so the wedding is next week? Perfect!" The 'Queen' exclaimed, very excited for the event. This will bring the Darklands under their finger, uniting the dimensions for 'peace.' The two, Earthland and Darklands, were the last ones left, and opposites.

Except, if the two were to combine, it would cause an apocalypse. Though, with how twisted reality was, people didn't pay attention to it. After all, with the current state of the world, if someone's will was strong enough, they could bring back their loved ones. Even if the reality were to perish, a change this severe would have lasting effects on the world, past, present, and future.

In another room in the palace, it was dark, with candles around the inside. Opening the door was the 'Ace', to see the 'Jack' waiting for them.

"You called for me?" The 'Ace' questioned, ready for whatever they had to throw at them.

"Do you remember that one time you caught me after beating up those thieves?" The bodyguard blinked, surprised to be here just for a conversation.

"Um, very vaguely, but yes." The 'Jack' walked up to them and touched their arm in an odd way.

"Ever since that day, I just couldn't stop thinking about y-"

"W-W-Woah! That's crazy! I just got a report from one of the guards in the back of the castle! I'll be right back!" The 'Ace' frantically responded, bolting out of the door as fast as they could.

Inside the throne room, the 'King' watched the town

from his huge chair. With all of the memories that he took from the people over the course of years, he made a utopia for the people and for himself. He darkly chuckled, leaning on his arm that rested on the chair.

"I know you're here, you two. I won't tell them about your arrival, mainly for your safety." He said, turning around the seat to face the two at the door. Madison pointed at herself.

"Me? Why me?" William put his hand in front of her, stopping her from asking anymore questions.

"What in the world do you think you're doing? Bringing people joy just for your benefit? What's the point in doing that?!" He demanded.

"I tried to rule over the Darklands, and you ruined it. So, I'll take over your own home. Why not accept what I gave you? All of your friends have." He began, showing multiple screens of their allies absorbed in the lie. "Even your teacher, the previous hero, got her wishes. I gave you your family, and I gave you your master. Why don't you want it?"

The two both finally thought about this. All of their friends were finally happy for once, and if he took it away, some of them would go back to suffering. Plus, he would still be ruling over them, unless they defeated them, which might be a task too big for them to handle at the time.

They don't even remember what happened the day before!

"We can decide what we want to do with our lives! You shouldn't decide what happens to us! Bringing back the dead just so people would want you to rule over their lives forever is wrong!" Madison spoke up. "We know what you've done. You've been manipulating us for years, and if you think we're going to listen to whatever you say, you're an idiot!"

"Taking our memories and using them for your personal gain is a bad idea. No matter what you do, there's always an outlier. *Someone* out there is going to see through it, and you were so unlucky that it had to be us."

"...You know what? There's a wedding going on in a week between Prince Jett and A----. All of the Darklands born are invited. You'll receive a Royal Ticket for the Royal Passage soon. If you can't stop us by then, you might as well kiss any further chances goodbye then." He finally responded to them. "Until then, no one will be able to get into or leave Cappy City. Good luck trying to get any more of your friends!" With a press of a button, the large double doors to the palace opened, which showed a barrier now surrounding the building, and another one around the entire city.

But before then, the two were teleported right to the city limits, where the barrier resided. Madison tried to punch through it, but to no avail.

"...Looks like we'll have to go home for now." William brought up, beginning to walk into the direction of Madison's house.

"You're really lucky that he decided to do this now and that my house is right outside of town." She sighed, following him there. It looks like they were defeated now.

But will they be able to come to a decision...?
Let their friends live their perfect lives under an evil ruler, or defeat the ruler but return to how bad it was previously?

....

"Mom! We're home!" Madison exclaimed, walking in the house and closing the door behind them. There wasn't a response, leading to the tenor believing that she vanished because of her rejecting the reality. Then again, she didn't know if she was a dead person in the first place. She could barely remember meeting her sometime recently, before today.

Before she could continue speculating, said mom

came running out of a room, looking disgruntled to an extreme, catching her breath. Madison nor William could tell if she was just run over or if she got into a fight with someone.

Her partner, whose name hasn't reached either of them, came out of the room as well, equally disheveled.

"...I...made...dinner...!" Her mom told her in gasps of air.

"...Can I ask what happened?" Madison questioned them.

"...Sparring...match..." Her friend explained, then the both of them falling onto the ground, passing out. The two reality rejecters started to panic, thinking it was something bad.

Minutes later after running around, looking for something to wake them up, and Madison trying her poor attempts at healing them, they finally came to.

"What happened?!" The tenor asked them, hoping that they didn't run into any weirdos.

"All we did was have a quick fight while you guys were gone! Nothing else happened..." Huh, that did kind of explain things. While she had no idea what power her partner had, they both did kind of look banged up.

"...was it really necessary?" William asked them.

"W-We hadn't fought each other in so long that we just wanted to test each other's strength! That's all!" Madison's mom stumbled to explain.

"Why in the house, though...?" Her daughter mumbled to herself, then shook her head. "Nevermind that! We need to tell you something!"

....

"But yeah! Your mom sure does pack a punch!" Her

mom's partner started patting her back repeatedly. "Those 'Power-" Madison's mom smacked her, one hit able to knock her into the side of the wall.

"Stop trying to tell them your bad jokes!" She yelled. "...I'm gonna have to get that fixed."

....

They explained the state that everyone was in, and how it was really different from before. They told them how they knew that their memories were tampered with, but couldn't remember anything at all from the day before. The current situation with the big castle in the middle of the city, which they were now locked out of. They also brought up the encounter they had with the 'King', that name bringing them to their senses once for all.

The truth of the reality had been revealed.

All four of them finally remembered what happened the day before, and let's just say that it didn't sit right with a particular Zero holder…

"So we just have to go around, try to bring people to their senses, and expect them to listen to us? We only have a week!" Madison complained, not keen on doing this. The tenor didn't want to interfere with their happiness, but at the same time, didn't want to be ruled over for the rest of her life. "I don't even want to think about how those idiots were against us from the beginning!"

"It's not anyone's fault that they managed to do that, but I'm surprised that they could do that without slipping up." Her mom, name still escaping her, replied.

"I know that since they can change and take memories, most, if not all slip ups would be erased. Wouldn't there be something that would've raised question marks?" Her friend brought it up. After just getting that part back, she remembered…

"Isn't it a bit weird that out of all people, Allie is the one who has the evil Epitomus counterpart?" Chloe asked Madison. They were strolling through a nearby forest to the Band Houses, a bit before the City of Gold situation started. "If anything, I'm pretty sure I would've had the evil one, haha!"

"Now that you mention it, it is kind of weird. But she is the princess of the demon race, the one that tried to destroy the Earth." She joked as well. "But I wouldn't stress about it. It's probably just a coincidence…Wait, wasn't the Epitomus Kelli Squad evil too?"

"I wouldn't worry about that right now…"

"…Yeah, there was. We didn't take it seriously though." Madison sighed. "What were we supposed to do, though? Treat her as a suspect in a game we didn't even know about?"

"That's all in the past right now. What we do need to be worrying about however, is what they're going to be doing with this power they have over the public." Her mom warned them. "Everyone else is absorbed in their own delusions, and now there's a barrier around the city that we can't get through. Unless you two can get to people by other means, you can consider this all over."

"There's that Royal Passage thing, but highjacking it constantly might alert them. We'll need to get someone over there to convince them, while we get the others outside of it." William told them. After thinking for a few seconds, Madison smirked.

"…I have just the idea."

Chapter 21

OPERATION: WEDDING CRASH

The Darklands people are out of the question. We can't tell any of them about what's happening, not even James. That also means we have to try and get through to them on the day of to save us from fighting more people. The wedding is in two weeks, and we can't get into the Cappy City limits. Which means, our only option is to call people stuck in the town.

Of course, trying to let people know they're living a lie over the phone is not that effective. We don't have any other choice, though. The Royal Passage is only going to go through once in time for the wedding. So, with William on board, he can convince them on the way. Whether that be by force or by just talking doesn't matter, what matters is if he could get through to them.

While the exact details of the party aren't going to come to me, there's definitely a way for me to find out. Inside knowledge. Chloe is definitely going to be there, as she used to be a *villain, lives with the best hero ever, and is also stuck in the city. So, let's see if she has any time to talk to me…*

....

After a long hour of talking on the phone with her, I managed to get this:

There will be two parties. One to celebrate the 'marriage', and one after it to finalize the contract where the two would be wed, uniting the two dimensions for as long as the king sees fit, which would be forever. According to her, this is what was meant to happen. Since I know what this would really do, which is destroy both places simultaneously in the time span of a few months, I'm gonna dismiss that.

The 'special guests', ones with the Royal Ticket, are seated with top priority, coming in via the Royal Passage, a train that stops right in front of the palace, as it's the heart of the city. They board the train sometime around 11:00, and arrive around 30 minutes later, before the first celebration starts at 12:00. This means that the train goes through both force shields (only allowed entry in the entire city) in 30 minutes.

And since William is the only sane one with a ticket, that means he has to get through all of the passengers, and to the front car, in only 30 minutes. Thanks to Kendall letting me see his blueprints for the train, I know that in the front car, there's a control box. This box will break the first barrier. Mom's friend told me that she spotted a satellite dish near the back of the palace on her way to the house, so we have to hope that's for the second one.

I don't know how William'll sneak in after causing a ruckus on the train. That will probably come to my thoughts later. He just has to get through them, break the box, get out of the train and destroy the satellite dish. I highly doubt whoever's escorting them will be super duper ultra strong, but just in case, i'll tell him to be extra careful.

Whoever we have will sneak into the party, blending in with the people there. We'll have...someone give the signal to start the tear down. Maybe it'll be cool like, a look in the eyes that's the go ahead. Maybe there's going to be a fight between who gets to be with who! That sounds hilarious. 'No, I shall be the one to marry ____!' Then a huge battle breaks out.

Fight for love aside, I left my phone call with Chloe with a small wake up message.

'Does this seem...right to you? Is this what you really want?'

She's smart. They'll all realize it soon enough. I even asked Kendall the same question. They both used to be villains, after all. Now we have people who were 'good' and then turned rogue. We'll need all the help we could get.

I don't want to bring my mom into this, since I just met her the other day. It really feels like I know her. Maybe the reality was wrong from a certain point, and even I was oblivious to it. There may be laws that have been ripped out, a change in customs, changes in people's perception of things.

We're rising heroes, and I believe we deserve to know what the world actually looks like. Heck, even Ms. Stevens is out on the moon trying to normalize space travel. With what mom told me, it wasn't like that. Even with how fast technology advanced thanks to powers somehow coming in, the government put regulations on when and what comes out.

That's all I need to write...I think. I might come back to review this later.

Madison closed her Apple Juice Recipes book. Since Orange Juice Recipes had become way too full, she had gotten a different version. That was only what she wrote down for her plan, her thoughts had been running crazy ever since she could actually think for herself.

They really were betrayed by Allie, one of the top

three strongest people in their program, whether she was the best was debatable, but her showings at the Hero Festival... were certainly better than she was showing normally. Madison often wondered what else she did when Allie left to go on missions, now even more so.

They also were betrayed by Kandi. Almost completely unexpected. In the weaker house and the Kelli Squad Hideout blending in with the others, she was a great spy, Madison hated to admit. She should've found her recent friendly advances suspicious. From now on, her guard is going to be up.

How strong were they really? Should she train some more?

"I know you're here, you two . I won't tell them about your arrival, mainly for your safety."

...What did the King mean by that? Hopefully it's because of how strong they are. Madison didn't try to imagine what else could be going on. She was writing in her notebook on the couch next to her mom, who was watching the news. She glanced in the television's direction, hoping to focus on whatever they were saying. Great, yet *another* story about Kim.

"I guess her dream was to be overwhelmingly famous." Madison muttered, her mom nodding in agreement.

"I'm surprised Cook even allowed this dream to happen. He might have done it so people wouldn't think too much about what was actually happening." She responded, then turned down the volume with the remote. "So, if you don't mind me asking, what was your dream?"

"They had to ask people to collect it directly, right? Well, I think I said that I wanted my family. Based on what's altered right now, I didn't know I even spent any time with them." Madison told her, holding a pillow up to her chest. "I remember now that you had left on a mission, but I didn't know before the other day...huh, you look kind of young to be my mom. How old are you?"

"I'm physically 17 now, but you were born when I was around 21!" Madison's jaw practically dropped to the floor. 17...but 21 when she was born...how? "...Oh. I forgot to tell you about that. Listen closely, okay?"

....

"I have a task for both of you. This might be a bit risky though. Actually, very risky." The other version of King Cook, Mr. Cook in the past said to them. She and her partner nodded, waiting for him to continue. "You remember the story of the Legendary Crystals? When one of the users of the three original powers says the command 'Sun and Moon, join together with Power like how you have been forever,' and summons them, you're allowed one wish. To counteract it being used for non heroic deeds, all wishes have a consequence, right?"

"Yes, that's true. What about them?" Her fellow hero asked.

"We have them all located. This might sound crazy, but please listen to me. One of the rules in the Darklands disappeared right in front of one of our lookout's eyes. It used to be Rule 31, 'No matter how powerful the King shall be, do not abide by him if he wishes to combine Earthland and Darkland.' You and I both know that my counterpart has started losing his mind." He started, looking out the window. It was raining really hard outside of his office. The anticipation of what was next was almost unreal. "I have come up with a plan if he tries to cause havoc upon both worlds, and you have to trust me."

"...And what would that be?" Madison's mom crossed her arms, preparing for the worst. Were they going to do an undercover mission?

"I want you two to use the crystals to jump in time. About seven years, to be exact. The consequences of this kind of

time related stuff will be your bodies reverting to a younger state, and your aging might be a bit slower. By the time your kid is 14, you two will be around 17." He elaborated. Mr. Cook then went on into more specifics.

They will wait until her child is born for them to send them off, and the heroes will take turns raising them until they come back. When there are more suspicious sightings in the time that they're gone, they will fill them in on it. He assures her that she will make up for any missed time with their child when they arrive, judging by the nature of who they'll be raised by.

When the two of them were dismissed, they let out a much needed sigh. Leave for seven years on a mission based on a hunch? What in the world was he thinking?

"I really wanted us to be there for the first few years..." She told her partner, who rubbed her shoulder.

"It can't be helped. This might be for the best. Sometimes we have to lose something for the greater good."

....

"...and I guess he was right, because we're in the same situation over a decade later. Even if you don't remember, we did spend a lot of time with you when we came back. Because of how secretive the mission was, we couldn't spend a lot of time with you out in the open." She continued, chuckling a bit. "But, even when we were gone for half your life, you still loved us. Man, I still remember that look on your face."

"...So the other Cook guy is formidable too, huh. I hope this plan can at least stack up to half of what he came up with those years ago." Madison said, fascinated by the story. She then thought about the party again. How were they supposed to blend in with everyone else there? She didn't have any fancy clothes in her wardrobe. "Uh, mom?"

"Yes?"

"Can we go shopping? You know, outside of city limits."

Chapter 22

FINAL PREPARATIONS

Tomorrow's the day. With the week, Madison spent time mentally and physically getting ready for the fate turning event. She was finally allowed to take those bandages (that she changed constantly) off, freeing up small restrictions that were still on her legs. Being burnt directly by the flames of the underworld is no joke. She didn't know what to expect if it happened twice.

William had been preparing his own way, supposedly looking for 'the best allies.' Well, he doesn't have many options, since most of the people they could get to easily were from the Darklands. Madison hoped he wasn't joking and did something stupid.

She also learned a bit from her mom's friend. Her power was 'Energy Distribution,' an unclassified power. It's a lot like what '345' was. She had complete control over where her energy focused, how much there was, and how focused it was. Madison learned that the markings that appeared were simply visual effects, and she could get rid of them with no sweat.

When she was working with William, she went to her mom. Since she had the original 'Power' without any add-ons, she was a really great teacher for her. Apparently, Madison was one of the first in history to actually get part of the Legendary power from a parent. Usually, if the one who got it passed down had a kid, the kid would either get the other parent's power or something completely different. If there is a lack thereof, it would always be the latter.

Madison tried giving her friends more nudges in the right direction, uncertain if they'd even snap out of it. She probably did it enough to where when the time comes for her to say the whole truth, they'd listen.

This betrayal situation was getting on her last nerves. The rest of her friends were most definitely oblivious to it, so they're probably treating them with the utmost respect. Allie and...Kandi, right? Who would've expected them of all people? She'll need a disguise for them to not recognize her, and maybe a new name.

A name...no, not needed. Her most obvious features were the bandages, which were off. Everything else, like the scars, would be covered up by the suit she got. Her hair, the obvious bun, makes it two.

"Perfect." Madison smirked, looking at her bed. Right next to where she usually slept was the outfit. A black long sleeve dress shirt and pants, accompanied with a black vest, topped off with a blue tie. The store she got it from was hero oriented, so whatever accommodations were made to it were selected by her mom. All that was left was to mentally prepare.

....

"We can't." Allie said.

"Why not?" The figure asked her, leaning on their vehicle behind them.

"I'm engaged, remember? Jeez, Walter. Always trying to butt in on political affairs."

"I don't care if you're getting married. Us just going for a ride isn't gonna do anything to your match made above." He explained to her. "Besides, you know that the only person who'd be 'mad' about it is Jett. We've been through way more stuff together than how much time you've looked at him."

"That's not the problem. What if someone sees us?" Walter reached and grabbed Allie's hand.

"Then we'll just have to go a route that no one knows about."

....

Chloe stood outside of a store in a shopping center. It was named 'Tag's School Supplies'. She checked her watch.

"*Three o'clock exactly. It should be coming out right about now...*" she thought. The door opened next to her, the jingle catching her attention. Out came presumably the owner with a neatly wrapped package. He handed it to her with both hands.

"Your calculators, right?" Tag asked her, and she nodded, taking it. With it still wrapped, she investigated it by seeing how heavy it was. It was rather lightweight.

"Thank you again."

"Don't mention it." He walked back into the store. Chloe decided to walk back to her house.

In truth, Tag's School Supplies is a supply store on the surface. When you make a 'reservation order,' that's when it becomes a weapons shop. Tag is a bladesmith at heart, making all kinds of them. Chloe, who's weapon she materializes most often is a longsword, requested for a solid one of the same. This way she wouldn't have to waste that much energy.

....

Kandi shifted around in her chair, looking at something on the wall next to her desk. The room was near black, candles lit ablaze with her dark flames. She held up a glass bottle, whatever inside glowing despite the lack of light in the room.

"This one will definitely work." She dropped a power crystal inside, and it dissolved as if it was rock salt in water. It changed from a clear color to pink, a little bit of gas coming from the top of it. She closed it and shook it up. "It didn't when I tried it on her water that long ago."

She was certainly scheming something. Maybe something for the party, also? What does Kandi have planned?

....

Kim rummaged around her living space down in the City of Gold. She looked around for some more tools to pack for tomorrow, just in case. Explosives, all sorts of weapons, her favorite gun, and just about whatever she could fit in the hidden compartment Kendall made her.

"If what Madison said was true about this being a lie...I don't want to believe it, but I'm going to have to leave this paradise," she thought, looking out the window, and seeing a group of fans trying to find her house. Staring for a moment, she then closed the blinds to try and not be noticed.

....

"So, Mom, another question. Are you an underground hero?" Madison inquired, looking through Orange Juice Recipes. She overheard Mandy talking about it before, so she was interested in the concept. The unknown heroes, saving lives while in the shadows.

"Yes, I was in the system since high school, and since I have to go through high school again, I'm in it again. You want to learn more?" Her daughter eagerly nodded. "Well, the name 'Underground' is because of our focus on missions. Unless we're needed to, we rarely go out in big groups. Our main code is secrecy, which is why it took awhile for you to find out it existed. There's also…"

Her mom went into another explanation. This system of heroes is mostly made up of high schoolers. They either choose the regular program, where they could work under each heroes' various organizations, or this one. Getting into either requires a license, which they try out for in the entrance exams, or they get recommended and tested to prove their trust. The entrance exams, also known as the hero exams, are taken by anyone interested in joining. There's a written portion and a fighting portion. There were instances where some scored high enough on the written test to get in, and vice versa.

Inside the program, the high schoolers are separated by sections. The cover up for the Underground Heroes is the marching band. Each section has their leader(s), and they are all masters of instrument combat. To become a Drum Major, a high position in the system, you must master the different fighting styles. There are exceptions to it, her mom specifically mentioned the newly implemented 'Bari Style.' Some have sub styles that you must show your hard work to learn, such as 'Piccolo Style.'

"…Since I'm pretty sure you haven't met Vic yet, I guess I can teach you a thing or two on Sax Style. I recall a friend of yours saying 'Impact!' as an attack, right?"

"Yeah, Brandon said that a lot. What about it?"

She went on to explain how Saxophone Style worked. It is a fighting style that involves charging an attack by repeatedly punching. Something almost like an air bubble will begin circling either of the user's fists, and will increase in strength and size depending on how much they charge. If enough, it could be anywhere from a small blast to a huge one.

Brandon never used the projectile side, and was rather impatient on how he used it. Sax Style is all about patience, and with that comes stronger attacks. While his version was different and from his own power, this is one that can be used by anyone, regardless of if they have a power or not. The 'Impact!' part was just his style, and this is Sax Style. Her mom offered to teach her the fundamentals of the style.

"Take this paper. I want you to imagine this." She handed her a blank card. Madison took it, and closed her eyes. "You're punching...a wall. With each punch, the crack on it gets bigger and bigger, until eventually..."

"It shatters into pieces." Madison finished, squeezing the card tight. It was made of a surprisingly tough material, and didn't crumple up. Eventually, she gave up, letting out a sigh. "Ugh, I can't get it!" She complained.

"It's okay, not everyone gets it on their first try. This is just the first step. Why don't you give it another shot?" Madison closed her eyes again, visualizing herself punching the wall again.

If the process to summon the bubble is by attacking a bunch, then an equivalent to that would be tapping the paper a lot. It's way too small to fight, so I have to compensate.

Her mom watched as wind gradually gathered around the hand that held the card, until it was big enough to surround her entire hand. Madison opened her eyes, and saw that the bubble had appeared.

"So, you said I could throw it, right?" Her mom nodded. She looked around, then spotted a tree stump. Madison threw it, and once it made an impact, it exploded. While the explosion itself wasn't huge, it still definitely did damage.

"Super impressive! Not everyone can do that in a day. It's usually a week-long process." She told her, clapping in applause for her. Madison felt like she was extra prepared for tomorrow. She'd have to get in contact with William early in the morning to see what he was up to. The King definitely had a bunch of speeches in store for them, and there was probably a long battle to go down in the history books.

...She may have underestimated the stakes behind it.

Chapter 23

HIJACKING THE TRAIN

10:45.
*15 minutes before the train arrives and takes in its
passengers outside the first barrier.*
The Plan: Get on the train while William executes his idea.

Madison straightened her tie, bringing her watch closer to her face. She looked at the train from a nearby alleyway. With the blueprints, she saw that there's a bubble surrounding the entire train that allows it to pass straight through, and into the heart of C Town. It's big enough for her to sneak around the top of it, and she won't have to worry about people seeing her with how fast it's going.

"So, how's it looking on the inside?" She said quietly. On her watch was William's contact. In the train, he was in the last cart, sitting down in a seat.

"It's clean, but I guess that's not what you're asking. Train got here early with a few guards and one. No clue why they were stationed on this ride but they're here, so I'll keep that in mind. Everyone except for Jett and James are on the list, being that they got here a day before." He told her. "No one's gotten here yet, so let's wait a few minutes."

Once William confirmed that everyone had gotten on a few minutes later, Madison snuck around the street to climb up the ladder on the right side, and she sat down on the roof.

"May the first plan commence."

11:00. 30 minutes before their arrival at the palace. Plan - Deal with everyone on the train to get to the first box. She gave the call, and he sat up from his seat, still calculating out a game plan. Both him and Madison were both strategists, two of the same kind. Since there wasn't a definite answer of who was in each cart, he'd have to be careful and creative with each situation. And in the first car...

....

"Oh, hey Kim, haven't seen you around that often. Why's that?" William opened up, getting closer to her with each step. She crossed her arms.

"It's because I've been busy with interviews and parties. I saved the world a little while ago, you know!" Kim proudly stated. "You must've never heard! Kinda shocking, since it was all around the news. I'm the savior of the City of Gold and the One's Above, so I'm really famou-" William reeled back and punched her across the face as hard as he could, taking out a bottle of hand sanitizer from his pocket and using it on his hands. Kim laid on the ground, knocked out cold.

"Ugh. I don't want to listen to that. Waste of my

time." He opened up the door to the next car. Not wanting to possibly lose any more minutes, William immediately cut to the chase once he closed the door and got in completely. He put his hands together and pulled one arm closer to him, creating a bow made out of pure energy, pointing it right at Bailey. "Sleep Shot." Before she could make any decision, he put her to sleep using the energy arrow. He went straight into another one, noticing it was just a bunch of guards.

William kicked each one of them as hard and as fast he could, not wanting to alert *one*. The bigger one of them all stood towering in front of the door to the other side, so he leaped over him (a tight fit between the roof and them), and kicked their head, and dropped all of them. He looked down on his watch for the time, and saw that only three minutes had passed.

"How's it looking up top?" William spoke into the watch.

"First barrier is far from here, so just keep it up and we'll be able to get through."

"Roger."

"...Quit it."

He cracked a smile before stepping foot on the next car. Oh...It's his previous captain. They have so similar powers, that picking who would be in charge was based on a different matter. William is a master of Perfect Counter, constantly studying the technique when he previously thought he was powerless. Sid has the ability to copy anyones power, as long as he can touch them, and he knows the name of it. His observations must be on point for him to know exactly what to do.

Even with their almost two years together as captain and lieutenant, William never discovered Energy, the unclassified rank, until recently from training with his old master. The two had never met in person, and only through her logbook, and he didn't meet her until the false reality stuff began. While Sid studied each power frequently, there would be no conceivable way for him to know about Energy.

"You're challenging me?" Sid questioned, as he stood up to face him directly. He was a couple of inches taller than him, but he couldn't care less.

"Unless you want to let me through to the last one, yes, I am." He answered. With his copying abilities, he could try using them as much as he wanted to, but in theory, it wouldn't work. Unclassified powers are not documented anywhere officially, by anyone. Confident in his beliefs, William took out his energy bow. "Now, if you will." Sid raised his hands up in defeat.

"Fine, fine. You got me." Lowering his guard, he walked closer and closer to the door. William put his hand on the handle to open it. Suddenly, before he could pull it open, he felt a hard blow hit him square in the back. He turned around sharply to face Sid again, trying his hardest to not cough up anything. He noticed that he was a bit farther away, almost at the other end. As fast as William could move, he dashed straight towards him. Sid started to throw rapid punches at him, his first instinct was to block, but he began to watch his strikes closely.

When one punch took longer than the other, he immediately started punching as well, countering each one as best as he could. Each impact kept on getting more powerful. To counter it, William kept adding more and more energy to his strikes, and then finally decided to pour a lot into his foot. He jumped up to kick Sid straight in the face, sending his body straight into the roof. Because of the hard material it was made of, he fell back down to the ground.

"How was that, captain?" William asked, catching his breath. Normally each strike would've been the same, but he must've picked up Sax Style sometime recently. When he didn't answer, he hit him with a 'Sleep Shot' just in case. He shouldn't waste any more energy than he has to, because of who was in the final car. William checked his watch.

11:10. 20 minutes before their arrival at the palace.

"Oh. What brings you here, William?" The figure in front of him said. He frowned, now with his hands in his pockets.

"None of your concern. How do you know my name?"

"You were on the royal passage list, so I had to connect the dots! I'm not an idiot, you know." They waved him off.

"Why aren't you at the palace? Shouldn't you be getting ready for the wedding?" He asked. "...Allie?" She finally looked at him instead of watching the train's course.

"I got ready a few hours before. I just wanted to say hi to the special guests. I mean, you guys are from my fiance's home land." Allie's eyes darkened, her aura slightly visible around her. "And also, for your first question, how could I forget the one who saw right through my plan? That was about four years of hard work down the drain. Even when you guys found out I was the demon princess, who would think it was the unsuspecting, heroic prodigy?"

William's facial expression only deepened. She was right. Out of everyone there was, no one would've expected it to be her. It's only when she started asking people similar questions when suspicion was raised. He shook his head, going back to his neutral face. He shouldn't get distracted. The box was right in front of him, and that's what they came for. William noticed the faint view of the barrier. It was far away, but that means he had approximately 5 minutes.

She started by repeatedly firing blasts, William catching on the moment he saw the first one, and countered it with his own. When it started to become fruitless, Allie kicked at his right side, which he also saw coming, so he made an energy shield to block it. Once the impact wore off, William put the energy back into his body and sent it straight to his leg. Before he could attack, she beat him to it, kicking him again at her full strength. No weights, no rejection of true self, no set backs at all. He poured as much into it as he could to block it, but he could still feel one of the bones in his leg cracking. William grimaced, shook it off, and took out his shield again to block more strikes, planning in his head.

I really should've tried overestimating her power, because that was a hard blow. I can't counter something I can't match the strength of. Hate to admit it, but she's a bit too much for me right now. Then again, all I'm here for is the box.

William pushed her back as hard as he could with his shield, immediately turning it into a bow. Once he spotted the power box, he pulled back and shot at it, destroying it completely.

"So that was your idea, huh? Well, I guess your plan worked." Allie told him after glancing at the box. "This fight isn't going to go any further. I'm not going to waste my time on y-" He had already gotten out of the car, the noise of the top hatch closing stopping her from going on.

....

11:14. 16 minutes before their arrival at the palace, 1 minute before they reach the second shield. Plan - Destroy the second box to allow non invited people through the barrier. One minute remaining.

Aiming straight for the castle, Kim flew, screaming from the velocity. She can't normally float or fly, so things like this are new to her. Madison had intentionally missed the place, trying to land her right behind it, which worked perfectly. The clarinet crashed straight into the ground, struggling to get up from being dizzy.

Eventually, she stumbled over to the very obvious satellite dish. You would expect such an obvious blindspot to be heavily guarded, but it was the opposite. No one was in her line of sight. Kim simply kicked the box until it was visibly dismantled, and watched above her to see the barrier flicker, until it eventually fell. She sighed in relief, heading over to a building. She was sure happy to not have to deal with anyone in this mission of hers.

"I was hoping that Madison would've shown up. Oh well, sometimes you just have to settle." A voice said behind her, which sent chills down Kim's spine. She hesitated in turning around, but had to. It was none other than Kandi. She remembered her being a part of the Kelli Squad, the ones that interrogated her back in the Darklands. What was she doing here?

....

William joined Madison up top, the two of them sitting down.

"That last fight sounded pretty rough. Are you doing okay?" When he actually thought about it, he winced, feeling the pain in both his leg and his back. "...I'll take that as a no. We'll get Chloe to patch you up when she gets convinced completely. For now, take these bandages to at least stop it." In her back pocket, she had a small contraption that when she pressed a button, it turned into a bigger bag. Madison gave him what he needed, and looked back at the shield.

"Still up, isn't it?" William questioned. She nodded. "At this point, let's just hope whoever can think can get through with this." They both heard footsteps from on top of the carts. Thinking it was the enemy, they immediately got ready to fight. But, it was just Kim.

"H-Huh? What's wrong?" Madison asked her, while she was catching her breath.

"T-Throw..." The tenor blinked.

"...What?"

"Throw me! Quick!" The saxophones exchanged glances, and both shrugged. Madison grabbed the back of her shirt.

"Prepare for takeoff!"

When Kim first woke up, a note was next to her body, giving her instructions to go find something behind the castle and destroy the power box. She knows that Kandi is reportedly working alongside the king, who had graciously invited her into the palace for her recent brave acts. Something deep inside her told her not to trust her...

"Uh...hi?" She managed to say. So much for bravery. Kandi chuckled a little.

"Hello, Kim the Savior. You got here early, way faster than the train."

"Oh! My followers have brought me here with this new technology that can teleport. There's teleport stations around cities now." Not completely a lie. Said technology did exist, and her followers did escort her to the Royal Passage.

"If that's the case, then you can continue doing what you were doing. Don't mind me. I'm just a guard." Kandi then walked away. Kim let out another dramatic sigh. Though she doesn't remember her being strong, she wanted to be extremely cautious.

．．．．．．．．．．．．．

William was...shocked to say the least. While he didn't exactly think of this to be a cakewalk, him being kind of badly injured by only the first step was almost a wrench in his complete plan. Just one hit from Allie alone with her fully realized strength was enough to fracture something in his leg.

"Okay, so how are we gonna get me in? I wasn't invited, and he was dead set on keeping me out." She asked again, wanting to get him to retell this part of the plan before they got there. Madison, despite this fate deciding day, still can not remember things for the life of her.

"Based on how Kim managed to break the box, they're likely pretending to not know what we're doing. We both know that they clearly hate us, so they must be keeping up appearances by inviting me. As for you, they might have known we were planning to get on the train, so…" He went on to tell Madison that he wouldn't put it past them that she probably would be allowed in. Them denying her entry isn't a smart move.

....

"How do I look?" Jett asked Walter. The two of them had decided to make sure they looked presentable before this dance. The prince knew the king might be looking, so he went against wearing traditional Darklands garb and decided with a suit he found in an Earthland store.

"Great. I'm sure she'll love it." Allie was head over heels for the poor knight, even having just met him only a few weeks earlier. Jett was still worried about doing this, but he really had no choice, and had to just sit it out. Walter patted his shoulder trying to comfort him, breaking him out of his thoughts. "Don't worry about it too much. Everything's going to be alright."

"…Okay."

Chapter 24

INVADING ENEMY LINES

Slipping into the event itself was no challenge. The second she heard a door open in the back of the building, she snuck into there. It was certainly a party. No lights aside from the disco lights, loud blaring music, dancing. Madison looked around the place, seeing the tables on one side of the room and the 'dance floor' on the other. She put on some sunglasses and hoped for the best, despite the dark interior.

The problem was trying to avoid people. This was technically trespassing, as she had no clue if she was invited to the actual party itself. Clearly there would be some form of guest list that whoever was at the front would be over. With how big the venue was, she expected a lot more people to be in here once the party started.

Madison spotted William sitting at one of the tables, and shot him a thumbs up. He noticed, and returned it. He was certainly bold to sit there, considering that he had just beaten up a few of the guests on a train, and challenged one of the King's adversaries and gave her a *little* trouble.

Focused on that, she didn't notice a certain person walk up to her.

"What're you doing all alone at a party like this?" They asked, the voice catching her off guard. It was definitely Kandi. The dress she had on was certainly not battle appropriate, so Madison lowered her own guard a little. Maybe she didn't recognize her...thank the One's Above for her choosing to change her hairstyle up! Wait, maybe it's the glasses...

But, being against the wall with her arms crossed might be attention drawing. This could be a good opportunity to maybe get out there and learn some insight about the kingdom. She only had a few hours.

"Not much. I'm not well versed in Earthland customs like these." The ultimate scapegoat; pretend to be from the Darklands. Being around Kennedy definitely helped in this endeavor. She laughed at what she said. Madison didn't know whether she should be nervous about that or not.

"Well, with both lands joining, you might have to get used to it. What's your name?" Quick, think of something... something inconspicuous!

"Jewel." She remembered someone's name she met recently that started with a J, but not who. Presumably the effects of the Ideal Reality.

"That's a nice name. My name is Kandi, and I'm from here. I work directly under the king." Feigning surprise, she lifted up her eyebrows.

"Really? I've heard good things about him, but I've never worked under him. I was just employed under James." Kandi seemed genuinely interested in what she was telling her. Madison kind of felt bad for lying to her, but this was for her safety.

"What division are you in?"

"Flute."

"Wow, I play that too! Are you good at fighting with it?"

"I guess you could say that. I started training with it a few years ago, but got recently accepted. The process was way easier than I thought it would be."

"Oh, are you strong?" They bounced questions and answers back and forth from each other, and somewhere in between that, the underling went and got her a drink from that punch stuff. She drank a little, trying to find a taste. It was dangerously sweet, disturbingly so. There was no other way you could describe it. Sure, Madison had a sweet tooth, but this was way too much. Even more so than shaved ice in December.

She watched William just to see what his reaction to it was. He didn't think much of it himself, but Madison *knew* he hated sweets. Apparently it wasn't sweet to him, as he simply put it to the side. Time to test this theory.

Madison gulped the entire contents of the plastic cup, which apparently surprised her...date? What exactly were they doing together...

"I'm gonna go and get some more." Using the cup as a scapegoat, she went over to the table where it was without looking back. Madison took the ladle and poured some, drinking it. Now it tasted regular...odd.

'Maybe she has a different kind...' was her first thought, until she realized that was the only drink over there, aside from the coolers full of sodas and waters. Madison felt someone tap her shoulder. It was none other than Kandi again. What did she have to say this time?

"Meet me outside for a second." Now, this was certainly a different tone to their previous conversation. If it wasn't for the added effect of her whispering in her ear, the Zero user would've brushed this off and agreed without a second thought. Heart pounding with nervousness, she shakingly agreed,

"S-Sure." Madison followed her outside, trying to pretend to not know her way around the place. They probably planned out everything about the venue, escape routes and all. Kandi opened the door to the emergency exit, the one that the tenor had snuck in before. Okay, now she was really nervous. What was she gonna say?

The obnoxious pounding she heard in her ears was starting to get real annoying, and faster by the second.

"I know what you're here for, Madison. To interrupt the joining of the two dimensions." Her heart dropped, and her heartbeat had subsided, but she could still faintly hear it. The Zero user's sight started to get a little blurry.

"Yeah, so what? Gonna rat me out? That'll be great, actually." She spoke up, trying to intimidate her. That nonchalant look twisted into a slight, sardonic smile. Kandi put a hand on Madison's shoulder, her intentions of this action unknown.

"How about we make a deal? You wouldn't want to alert the king, right?" The offer was sure alluring, but why would she even ask? Is she rebelling against him? What's her deal…

More and more questions raced through Madison's head at once, but she decided she shouldn't leave the other hanging.

"And the catch is?"

"You have to dance with me."

"…What?" Was the first thing she got out. Dance with the enemy? *Why* would she accept that? Why is Kandi even asking her that?

But, she couldn't necessarily deny her either. Madison hated to admit it, but the girl had her backed into a corner. She had her wrapped around her finger now. Plus, there was no telling how powerful Kandi really was, because of how she had lied to all of them in the past.

She clutched her head. That was starting to hurt too. *What was this about? The punch…?*

"Fine. I'll play along." Madison replied. She watched Kandi trail her hand down her entire arm, then retract it.

"I'll see you inside then." The tenor stood in relative silence, mentally preparing herself for what comes next. When 'The Jack' had left, she checked the time on her watch.

12:15. Plan - Begin the takedown soon.

While she was against doing anything of these sorts with the enemy, it was necessary to do it. Kandi might be scheming on her downfall in the long run, but agreeing with her pushes back the inevitable battle, no, war, in the near future. Ignoring the monstrous headache she had, Madison went back into the building. The time was close.

．．．．．．．．．．．．．

"Are you okay?" Allie inquired, sat down at the table. The only other person there was Jett, right next to her. "You've barely talked to me all day."

"I thought that was how it was supposed to be." He first said, but then sighed. "Sorry, I'm just really nervous."

"What for?" Jett assumed she didn't know exactly what she had just asked. They were literally about to be *'married,'* and King Cook would join the two worlds together. The concept of both happening at the same time and being correlated was hard to wrap his own mind on. How was she not affected in any way by this? To him, the princess looked like this was just another day.

All except for that last bit, the prince brought it up to her. Allie nodded at every point he made. "It's not exactly the worlds I'm worried about, it's how people might think about us." She answered, and continued on, yet Jett tuned it out. The world might be nearing its end soon, but Allie cared more about public image…?

....

Walter watched them converse from across the room, wondering what they were discussing. They had initially left him to go dance, but went to their table. During that, he relocated to a different place in case they needed space. To be fair, they were getting married that day, and had just met maybe weeks or months ago. Luckily, James was at the table also.

"Not going to dance?" Death's son asked. After all, even since the party started, he had just sat in the same spot on his phone.

"Don't feel like it. Plus, I have a bad feeling about this whole thing." The younger king told him. "There's so much going on in one day, one place. Nothing small either, a lot of big things."

....

A slow song came on, and Kandi thought this was a perfect time to get her part of her deal, dragging poor Madison out to the floor. She wasn't too happy about leaving her drink behind, but the tenor knew that if she objected the plan would be toast.

"So…what brought this idea up?" She asked the question to try and fill in the blanks. This was something the Zero user needed to know. The flute's hands already found their place, while Madison didn't know what to do with hers. They didn't have much of a relationship before she kind of started training with her…

Back with the original, initial Band House, the two

had lived in the same flute room, their beds next to each other. Sure, they interacted back then, but not as much as they could've. Kandi never got the order from Cook to befriend anyone specific, but only to lie low. In truth, if their circumstances were normal, Kandi would admire the tenor a lot. Sure, she does now, but in a more twisted fashion.

The root of her obsession has no definitive cause.

Even when she trained her, they didn't have many opportunities to do so. But they spent a little quality time together. Except for that moment when she had to talk a little sense into her about heroism. Madison was out of commission for some time after that, but they still talked a little.

Sometime before that, Kandi tried attempting to brew a potion to use on her, but Madison deemed it as 'tasting horrible' and wasn't affected. This may have happened again, judging the punch tasting different the two different times Madison drank it. Sure, it had an effect, but not the one Kandi was intending, presumably.

The flute's wish was to have the one she loved the most as close as possible to her. Because the tenor's will was stronger, she wasn't put under her, but a different version of her was. Loyal to the one she served, yet her personality still clashed with it.

"You know, I've always admired you. The strongest power, tactical skills, and you're pretty strong. What more is there to ask for?" Kandi rests her head on Madison's shoulder. Her headache had subsided, now trying to will herself to stay attentive during this moment. The tenor clutched her shoulder while determinately saying,

"What are you trying to do, win me over to your side? It's not happening." She was firm in her stance against their tyrannical rule over C Town. She felt a hand grip onto the back of her vest, probably in return to her own action.

"Not on my side, but right next to me. You don't have to fight for us, but I want you as my guard." Kandi replied.

Her nails were surprisingly sharp, cutting straight through the fabric and deep into Madison's skin. She grit her teeth, not wanting to draw attention. In an attempt to conceal it also, Kandi effectively cauterized her wounds with her power. The tenor noted that her flames were hotter, way hotter than Mandy's. "The real thing would be better than a fake, wouldn't you say?"

Said in a hushed whisper. Madison looked around frantically for William, spotting him. They made eye contact at the same time, and once he noticed the position she was in, almost got up to start the fight. She stopped him, shaking her head, and mouthing 'We'll start in a second.' Luckily, whoever was over the music stopped it.

"The ceremony will commence shortly. We hope you're enjoying your time here!" The music then continued, Madison sighing.

"S-Shouldn't we be heading to our seats soon?" The situation she was just in was nerve wracking, and she was glad she got spared by time. Kandi backed away from her just a little, disappointment showing very obviously on her face. The tenor shuddered.

"I guess so. We could always continue this later!" Madison sped out of there and found a seat with her name on it. It was strange, considering she was the enemy of King Cook, but was even more surprised to see Kandi's name right next to her. So much for a saving grace…

She sat down quickly, not wanting the marks down her back to be seen by anyone when the lights came on. Anxiously, she texted William to get ready, watching as Jett and Allie went up to the stage, along with the King and his previous 'son,' the King of the Darklands.

1:30. Plan - Takedown soon.

Zero.Hero.2: hey, i think it's time soon. stay on guard

Darklands.William: ok

....

"You know, according to the history of our place in this world, the Darklands and the Earthlands were together. Both places have their respective dimensions, which were also combined as well. The first power user split them, as it was deemed natural by the Land Above." King Cook began his long speech. William rolled his eyes, not entertained by his history lessons. "As previous king of the Darklands, and now a ruler of the Earthland, I have control over both worlds. Using my ability, I can join the two worlds together in a seven day process. If two significant figures from each respective land were to sign a contract, and if I was there to officiate the deal afterwards, I could theoretically start this process. Don't worry, this will be fine, as the two were in harmony and peace even while together."

"So, here's the contract, you two." On an altar, there was a piece of paper with a similar speech on it. At the end, it read:

By signing this, you agree with the other party to commence with the joining of two worlds. The Darklands and Earthlands will be, in turn, forever at peace.

Allie was quick to sign her signature, but Jett had a huge amount of second thoughts. He hesitated, pen shaking right in front of where he'd put it down. King Cook put a comforting hand on his shoulder, which at first made him tense up. He then looked at James, who gave him an enthusiastic nod, as much as the near silent kid could.

This was the push he needed. He signed off on it, and the king took the paper from the altar, now standing directly in front of them on the stage. They were now at the final portion, tension in the air extremely high.

"Finally, does anyone have any objections?" He asked

expecting no one to respond. Walter stood up to say something. This was his chance to take Allie away from Jett.

"I-" He was interrupted, however, by a huge explosion from the roof of the building, smoke spreading around that entire sector. The paper flew out of the King's hands, effectively ruining his plan. Two figures could be seen standing on the rubble of the destroyed wall.

"Sorry we're late to the party!"

Chapter 25

THE TRUTH

"Hey!" Amidst the chaos, Kim ran into the venue, getting Madison's attention.

"What?" She then alerted the tenor that the person at the front allowing people entrance looks just like her, and she denied Kim entry, despite being on the train. "Wow...that's certainly something." Was all she could reply.

On the stage, King Cook demanded,

"Who in the world are you two?!" He wanted to know who was the cause of interrupting the officiation of the worlds.

"I'm sure you know our names very well." A familiar voice to some of those spoke up. The smoke cleared, and it was revealed to be Mandy and Brandon, who weren't invited, but wanted to have a grand entrance. The two had no clue about the plan Madison had in place, though.

Brandon had on a red dress shirt with suspenders

over them and black slacks. Mandy was wearing a white dress shirt.

This was extremely convenient. Said Zero user pressed a button on her watch that changed her shoes to more comfortable ones, then took off her vest for more mobility. She ran over to where William was, standing next to him and taking in the surroundings. People were evacuating the building left and right, going through each possible exit imaginable. It was understandable, because the king sure looked like he popped a few screws loose.

He's been putting this plan into action for a few decades if anything. Taking anyone he could under his wings so they would listen to his plan without hesitation. Allie, a prominent prodigy, who was the adopted daughter of the number one hero, Ms. Martinez. She was the princess, technically queen of the demon race, which is what she pretended to deny. Kandi, the unsuspecting lower average fighter. How she was actually of prominence could've come as a surprise to anyone.

James, the upcoming captain of the clarinet division, who he adopted and made the prince of the kingdom. To make it not seem suspicious, he changed reality in the Darklands to make it seem like he's been in that position for a while. Jett, a kid who had very similar powers to him. Also to cover up, he made it to where he was his 'actual' son, letting him be the prince following James' mysterious treachery and absence.

In truth, he has influence everywhere.

"There's not a lot of people here. I'm sure that we'll out number his following." He spoke up, the other saxophone nodding.

"Number Divisions! Eliminate those teenagers!" King Cook exclaimed, raising his hand. On command, 10 groups of about 300 warriors came out of the back of the palace. They weren't far from the venue, as the two rivals could see them coming easily.

"Chloe, bassoon man, and William! Go and take care of those guys!" Madison exclaimed, the three going along with her plan and rushing outside. She was very glad that those three were nearby.

William and Kendall easily listened, eager to fight, the former not so much. Chloe didn't understand what was happening exactly, but knew she was on Madison's side, so followed her lead. With a tap of a button, she took out that new sword she had gotten from Tag's store. With a single wave of compressed air combined with her energy, she took out around half of one division. Kendall turned into his phoenix form and flew through an entire group, lighting them all on fire.He threw one of his gadgets at them, which heightened and spread the fire further around.

The tenor's partner in this endeavor summoned his bow and sprayed arrows directed towards one sector. If they didn't miss, they hit someone twice at two different points, putting them to sleep quicker than with just one Sleep Shot. Despite the strength inside one released extremely concentrated being high, the ones consecutively were comparable as well.

Madison then looked directly at King Cook. Today was the day she would finally face him. Suddenly, the fake version of her got in between her and Kandi, who she didn't realize was still there. She must really like her...

"Thanks for coming to my side, Madison!" The flute cheered, eagerly hugging her bodyguard. She maintained a stoic expression on her face.

"Sure." A simple response. The real one decided to challenge her first, knowing she would get in her way.

"So, what should I call you?" She asked.

"Ace. It's my role in this scheme."

"Alright." Madison kicked her straight in the stomach, then activating her 2nd Drive. Ace caught herself in the air, but not before a fist hit her straight in the jaw. The tenor wasn't going to waste any time with this. "Huh, you're pretty durable."

"I guess you're the one I should thank for that." She wiped the blood from her mouth, smirking a little. Kandi was very entertained by this exchange, watching with awe. Who would prevail, the true one, or the one summoned by her own volition?

...Unfortunately, that wouldn't be answered today. Shouting very loudly and revealing their presence, Mandy and Brandon appeared. With their combined strength, they both grabbed Ace's arms with one hand and dragged her away from the scene. This left Madison with Kandi once again.

On the stage, King Cook flew up to the sky, leaving James, Jett, and Allie. Walter charged forward, freezing Allie and landing on the ground.

"James, hit her with all you got! Don't hold back!" He shouted. His friend channeled all of the energy that he could in one final attack. He decided a lightning strike would be appropriate. With his sword, Jett flew towards Death's son and cut him straight across the chest. The pain distracted him from using his power. Allie broke free from his control, giving him a certain glare...

"I declare that we have a proper duel for the woman's hand." Jett stated, putting a hand on the princess' shoulder. He pointed his blade straight towards Walter, who rolled his eyes.

"Whatever, you're on."

....

Ms. Martinez and Ms. Stevens ran up to the palace, trying to get close to the palace. They were stopped by an invisible barrier. The former slammed her hand on it.

"We have to get closer! We can't leave them alone!" Ms. Martinez complained. On the other side of the barrier, Señora Salcedo and Ms. Barrels also attempted to, but it didn't work. Both parties attacked the barrier with all they could manage, but to no avail.

As it turned out, King Cook released a new ability from the air where anyone who was near his strength level could not get into the center of town.

"Must be unfortunate for them." He let out a maniacal laugh, watching them attempt to get in. The king might have to do this the hard way now, without his officiation.

Inside the barrier, the princess powered up, this time going all the way. No 50%, no limitations, full strength. This leveled the rest of the walls that were up in the building, blowing away all decoration. All that was left was the floor. Allie startled everyone, especially Walter and James, with this power.

"I'm still here." The latter said, putting his foot down. It shot a trail of ice towards the traitor. She jumped all around it, even when it reached her height in the air. It never caught her once. James got onto the ice and started skating on it, his jacket flying around in the wind. Once he felt he got high enough, he jumped up and turned the solid into water, sending it in her direction.

"I thought you were stronger than this." She taunted, flying straight through the water, her aura protecting her. Allie was way faster than he anticipated, and hit him head on. He held onto his stomach in pain, almost reeling over while she stood in front of him. James got her to back away from him by putting his hand right in her face, it heated up with him preparing to blast her at point blank.

Meanwhile, Walter was very engaged in his fight with Jett. The latter blocked all of his strikes with the flat of his sword, but rarely struck back. He was in a bit of a predicament due to the lack of darkness around him. This time, he wasn't even saved by his armor. But, he was very persistent in winning.

"The Earthland woman and I are bound together by fate and a contract! You can't change what's meant to be!" The prince exclaimed, swinging at him. Even with his gaping open wound, he got out of its way and kicked him across the face. Jett's sword clattered on the ground. He spat out blood, hitting Walter with his own fist.

"She was my friend first!" Death's son didn't bother with Time Control, fighting Jett fair and square in hand to hand combat.

William sighed, just using another large sum of arrows. There were just too many of them, and his leg was not having it. When he didn't see any focus on him, he kneeled down on his good leg.

"I don't see how anyone could even fight the king anymore, because of how strong Allie is. Something else is up here…"

Against the Ace, Brandon and Mandy were getting along well now, thanks to the reality in place.

"We really should've done this a long time ago, right?" Brandon questioned, using his Rocket superiority at his feet to launch himself. Mandy was following right next to him by using flames from her hands like propellers.

"Yeah, this is fun!" She responded, agreeing. Together, they could be considered an unstoppable force. The fake Madison was having a hard time dealing with them at the same time.

Kandi's wish created another version of Madison. Unfortunately, with how strong her power was, it couldn't be recreated completely. The tenor had exceptional willpower, enough to predict what was going to happen, and resist it with the right resources. The only thing the copy received was her lesser known ability, shockwaves.

It would be perfect if she was just fighting one of them, but that was not the case. When she grabbed Brandon's arm and sent shockwaves through his entire body, Mandy got in her way by giving her a blast full of flames, making her release her grip. Now smoking and charred, the Ace brushed some of the dust off of herself.

"I admit, pretty impressive. Try stopping this!" She moved the shockwaves downwards and into the ground, which caused something similar to an earthquake. Mandy and Brandon stumbled around, trying to stand their ground against her.

A wave of dark flames went past Madison, who barely dodged it, feeling the extreme heat almost graze her nose. She backflipped out of the way, and right before she landed on the ground, she activated Drive Three. The black lighting surrounded her, and the tenor flew headfirst towards her enemy. Kandi smirked, somehow managing to grab Madison mid air by her collar. She held her up slightly above her. The Zero user tried getting out of there, but it was dangerous with her fire ability, so she stopped struggling.

"This is your last chance. Join me, or fight against the three of us. Your choice." The previous flute traveler asked her. Madison nervously laughed in her face.

"If you're trying to scare me, it's not working." Noticing the position she was now in, it took her way back to when her friend, no, EP Allie in Karla's body, had her held over that mountain, and those flames surrounding her. Without thinking, the tenor headbutted Kandi. While she was complaining about how bad it hurt, Madison took in a deep breath, channeling the energy in her body. But with that fire still fresh in her mind, the hero froze in remembrance of those memories. The traitor gained her composure, grinning at the sight of her enemy's trance.

"I thought it wasn't working." Madison's vision

blurred in between the two times, and she tried with every fiber of her body to move forward and finish the job, yet she couldn't. The image of her entire body being set on fire. The red hot flames everywhere, taking over her line of sight.

Kandi wanted to finish the job, as she clearly denied her advances, but it was hard. She liked the tenor a lot, and seeing her in that state was horrible. *"Maybe things would be different, if I didn't have to listen to the King..."* She often reassured herself in the past, especially here. Kandi prepared a flame in her hand, trying to take this decision as slow as possible.

Madison came to her senses a little, able to see the imminent threat of the event happening twice. In a panic, the tenor jumped into the air. She took out her trusty canister and threw it to the ground, summoning her trusty stand. For unknown purposes she had the paper holding part taken off, and just replaced it with a flat metal slab.

"Thrust Zero: Homerun!" She yelled, swinging it as hard as she could. Kandi went flying in the direction Madison sent her, even going straight through the barrier.

Watching from above, King Cook was very disappointed in how this day went. With the contract missing and especially a lack of officiation, there was no joining of worlds. There wouldn't be another chance to do this either, especially with his and his lackeys' cover blown by Madison's antics. So, the only choice he had was to disable his Ideal Reality entirely. Almost like a gust of wind, the entire world was then changed to its last unaffected form.

Some people around the globe lost powers, even in the Darklands as well. Most of them had no knowledge on what was going down in the center of C Town, but they would eventually want to know what the reason for this happening was.

The truth was soon to be revealed.

....

Excluding William and Madison, they all came to their senses.

The former watched as his bow disappeared from his very hands, it flying away with the wind as bright blue shards. He should've known from the very beginning that it's suspicious when people who never had powers suddenly gained them.

He scoffed, brushing his shoulder.

"There's no point in me going on. I might as well just get out of here," William thought, walking away. In the middle of using his rocket ability, Brandon lost it and all momentum he had, falling face first into the ground. Mandy's flames died down by a lot. She turned off her power to help her rival up off the ground.

With a nod, the two silently agreed to just rush their enemy by running. Like sand on a windy day, she slowly disappeared into thin air.

"That was a nice battle. Well worth it, too." She said, smiling. Brandon and Mandy stopped dead in their tracks.

"...You know what's next?" The latter asked. Allie tried to use her mind control power, but it didn't work anymore. Once she learned from King Cook about how the royal lineage of the demon race had that ability, she wanted it too. Now, it is gone because of reality. James slowly caught his breath, having lost a lot of blood in a few minutes.

Jett and Walter were at a standoff, the former almost losing the fight. Then, they realized that they had been fighting for no reason. Both sad about it, they knew what had to happen now.

They had to defeat Allie, by any means possible.

"I wonder if you'll survive this!" Said princess' dark

energy enveloped her hand rapidly, having full intentions of defeating the king of the Darklands. That was until Jett stepped in between the two , stretching out his arms. "Oh? Do you have something to say?"

"...Screw you." Walter slowed down her releasing that blast by a lot to give his friend a chance to counteract it.

"Now's your chance!" James' hand was surrounded by sparks of electricity, concentrating in his fingers. Once he deemed it powerful enough, he pointed it straight at Allie.

"Say goodbye."

....

Mandy and Brandon, who both didn't have anyone to fight anymore, went after King Cook. Wind gathered around the Frost user's fist, and the Inferno user prepared her own attack. Not paying much mind to them, their enemy's cape began flowing upwards. Brandon got closest first.

"You ba-!" He shouted, before he was cut off with a hand grabbing him by the collar. King Cook slammed him on the ground behind him, then threw him in the direction of the palace. Well, what was left of it. Now it was just a normal capitol building. He did the same with Mandy, except just stopping her with his Darkness ability and tossing her in the same, vague direction.

Because the Ideal Reality was his creation, he wasn't affected by the strength change. This was his real power, and he allowed the others their chance to fight him. Now, they were all nowhere near him. The king heard footsteps and the tapping of metal on the ground drew closer and closer, turning to see who the sounds belonged to. It was none other than Madison.

"So, you're finally here to challenge me. I've been waiting for this for a while!" The tenor clutched her weapon, reeling back with both arms.

"You might've expected me to get weaker from you turning off that ability, but…" With a huge swing, the stand produced a huge wave of wind, some of it even strong enough to leave cuts in the ground and on his attire. "I've never felt any better!" King Cook, turned into his intangible form, spread around the entire area that the wind blew.

When it came to the Big 3, their battle was extremely difficult. It took the three of them for it to be feasible for Allie to lose. The princess would sometimes break out of Walter's control if she had the energy to do so. James was worn out from his fight with her earlier, but pushed himself past the limit numerous times. The drawbacks began to show, where his body couldn't handle the fire or lightning anymore. His body froze up, but not before…

King Cook turned the bright sky dark once he gathered himself together. If his master plan failed, he knew what he had to do.

Plan B was to forcefully merge the two worlds together, which would cost him his power. He would be the ruler of the land, and no one would dare to rebel against him, even without his main strength factor. He knew that if he rushed it, his life might be taken away, so the best time he could manage was a day.

With how weak everyone became, this would be a piece of cake. They weren't strong enough in the first place, so why would they be now?

As if time had slowed down, Jett breathed in. With their not being light outside, it was his time to dominate the battlefield. Allie chuckled, eyes glowing deep purple in the dark.

"You're finally going to give me a run for my money, huh?" She said, waiting for a reaction. Instead, he raised his sword up into the air.

"Illusion." He stated. In the princess' vision, the area became completely white, except for her own body. She looked down at her hands, and then around, wondering what he could be up to. Slash, cut. Numerous wounds from his blade appeared on her body out of nowhere, slowly. Red blood splattered on the blank ground. The prince was too fast for Allie to catch up with her sight.

In the real world, Walter kept her stuck in place while Jett bounced around her, striking everywhere he could. Eventually, he landed back down, lowering his sword.

"The Earthland woman will be stuck in that trance for a while. Let us go and take on the King himself." The other two nodded, James hardly able to stand.

"Taking me on, prince? I commend your efforts, but you won't be able to keep up with me." King Cook told him, keeping a stance. Jett held up both of his arms in front of him.

"Retribution." A black box came from the ground and contained the king inside of it. "You won't be able to use your power while inside. So, I'm going to stab you in the heart." He took his sword and went up to him, running it through the box and into his body. While it connected, only a small bit of blood was drawn.

"Not bad." King Cook grabbed the blade tightly and shattered it into pieces, then broke through the cage he was in. He prepared to punch him. "You'll have to try harder than that, though." Walter came in, carrying James on his back, and froze the King in his place. Taking the opportunity, Jett took control of King Cook's shadow and threw it up, which dragged him with it. Using that move again, he took him back down as hard as he could, creating a crater in the ground.

Jett knew that this wasn't the finishing blow, and that was confirmed when his previous ruler rose out by taking flight. King Cook tried blasting them, but Walter brought out his shield and blocked it completely. Dealing with the onslaught of darkness energy, he didn't notice when his enemy dispersed and appeared behind him, and hit him *and* James with another one.

When it was over, the king of the Darklands fell off Walter's back, fading in and out of consciousness. Jett tried to move him away again, but couldn't anymore. He was now serious. "You'll regret ever turning against me!" He exclaimed, using Jett's same move against him. He knocked him into Death's son, and then controlled both of their shadows to send them into the same direction, not caring where they went.

King Cook looked down at James, who was barely able to return the glance.

"...N-No matter what you do, you won't beat us." He stuttered out, coughing up blood. His previous master hovered his foot above his body, about to slam it into where Allie had injured him greatly earlier. A thin metal pole came out of nowhere and hit him straight in the face, making him stumble backwards.

"How dare yo-!" He was cut off by a purple and black aura that went at his feet, which he hardly got up in time to jump and dodge. It was none other than Madison, who clutched her damaged arm from using this without Drive Four.

"Darn it, I missed it. It would've done so much more." She complained. It did a lot of damage, as it left a huge trail through the ground. The tenor looked around, watching Chloe and Kendall still hold off the remaining warriors. Madison also noticed all of her friends scattered around the battlefield in varying degrees of damage dealt.

"By defeating you, my plan will definitely come into fruition. No more of your power around and it'll be smooth sailing from then on." He said, staring the young hero down. "Or, you could be my right hand man, my vice captain. Without Allie or Kandi, there's a few spots open. Together we could rule this place, won't you agree?"

"...True." Madison spoke up, but then clenched her fists. "I don't want to live knowing that I'm a part of your bullcrap grand scheme! Forget it!" King Cook sighed, shrugging.

"So sad. You would've been the perfect teammate..." In a blink of an eye, the ruler punched her straight in the stomach. "Disable!" He poured a huge amount of *his* energy into *her* body, which started from her core and went straight down. She felt her ability to use her legs leave her control by the second, then searing in pain. Before it reached her feet, however...

"Madison!" A voice shouted, getting both of their attention. Two figures came from the sky, one of them holding a glowing object in their hand. They teleported to King Cook's location, placing it on his back. He froze up, realizing what they were doing. It was a Power crystal, and it felt like electricity shooting through his veins. The king was enveloped by raging sparks from an electric field. The tenor collapsed, but was caught in the arms of someone familiar, and was teleported a bit away.

"...Mom? You came?" She muttered, looking up at her. The smile she gave set her at ease.

"Yes. My friend and I got in using the crystal to open a hole in the barrier. Now, with his power being disabled by her, the world is going to change." Her partner continued to stab it into him, draining his energy completely. The sky returned to its bright blue color. The barriers disappeared, and the four strongest heroes came in from the different sides, trying to get there as fast as they could. Her mom's friend took back the crystal , and let him hit the ground hard. "It's what he deserves for using a similar attack on you. I'm so glad I got here in time."

Madison felt her mom hold her tighter, and she loosened in her arms. *She was safe with her.* The pain that she actually was dealt came in full force, and the teen felt a wave of exhaustion come over her.

"So you two must've been the masterminds of this plan!" He yelled, despite not having a lot of strength left. "I wouldn't have expected less from Julia and Rose! Plus, why haven't you disappeared yet! The reality should have been gone minutes ago!"

"Shut up." Rose kicked him in the arm and watched him writhe in pain. After getting that satisfaction, she went over to Julia and Madison, kneeling down to the two 's level.

"We're going to let you deal the final blow, okay?" Her mom spoke softly, laying her down onto the ground.

"But I can't move my legs!" She protested, crawling over to get at least a good view of the king.

"There's a secret about your power that I think you should know. You'll be able to figure it out yourself, because of the Ideal Reality being gone." Madison's mind raced, trying to think of a way she could walk. She raised up her right arm, the one that wasn't messed up by her using a bit of Drive Four.

She took in a deep breath, and focused on the task on hand.

The tenor pushed herself up by her arm, hobbling on her legs and struggling to keep them from giving out. Her mom and friend watched in disbelief. Even though they were shaking sporadically, her legs kept her body up.

"I know that my power is similar to my mom's friends, and her too. So, I'll use my energy to…" Madison envisioned herself using a grappling type ability. Testing this theory, she shot out a stream of energy that had a hand at the end, and

grabbed the king with it. Lifting him up, she slowly brought up her left hand and pointed it towards him. It shook greatly, but she knew she had to do this.

"Power Blaster!" She put her hand on the flow of energy, and pumped all of the amount she could manage into it. Once it reached the last part, it exploded continuously around him, so she put her head onto the ground. "Finally, it's all over." Madison said with relief, feeling her body being picked up gently.

"This may be the last time we see each other, so listen closely…"

NEW BEGINNINGS

The world has returned back to its normal state. No changing reality by the minute, no big evil terrorizing villain from a different land. So now, there's a fresh restart for anyone. A perfect opportunity to settle down, and take a breather.

Powers. Some are born without them, and those with them have the innate nature to use them. They just know when the time comes when it's revealed during their childhood. For others, it's early, and sometimes it's late. Sure, the power ranking system exists, but it's outdated. Now, they're classified by rarity.

Your power is randomized, but you have a chance at getting one parent's, or even both. There are numerous varieties possible. You could meet someone in your area that has an extremely similar power to you around your age. The 'power wheel' resets every decade, and it's feasible for more and more to be added as time goes on.

'Power Wheel' theory is rather complex, and is still being studied to this day. The general consensus is that it's a randomizer wheel with millions, perhaps billions of different powers that anyone could be born with. It's where most people got their special ability, and someone who got it from their parents is very hard to come by.

Nico was a bit of a rarity.

Julia, their mom, was the 4th generation Power user. It skips generations by a lot and rarely shows up, but for this instance, it was right after her own.

Power is the greatest power for numerous reasons. It's special in a sense that whoever has it can learn and master any ability they want to. This was granted to them by the 1st generation Power user, Xenos, as he was the originator of all powers.

Rose also gave them some of her DNA, which ended up with them receiving both powers. Mastery over energy and complete control with it, plus the possibility of learning any power they wanted to. The theoretical *perfect* child created by the two would have so much potential. They could reach heights unseen before, perhaps even as strong as Xenos himself.

If Nico had learned this ability when they were younger, they would've been very cocky about having it. So, in a sense, the Ideal Reality helped them out sort of. Not in every way, though.

In a month, James had a full recovery from his injuries against Allie and King Cook, those two now imprisoned by the top four heroes. Well, #3 and #1 resigned. Kandi was also there with them, but they were in separate buildings across Earth.

Jett returned to his post, becoming King of the Darklands in place of King Cook. He often got visiting requests from Allie, but those were denied in a heartbeat or ignored.

He and Walter were frequently in contact with each other, the former going out of his way to visit him occasionally.

William's injury healed, but not completely yet. Even though he wasn't the recipient of a full beat down from Allie, it was nothing to sneeze at. Mandy moved away to the school that Brandon went to, enrolling in their hero program. They could not live without each other, it seemed. So did Amy, in pursuance of a better challenge.

Held in her arms, on the ground, Julia spoke calmly to Nico. It was a conversation that only her, Rose, and themself could hear. To not raise suspicion, Nico would be sent to live with one of their younger allies. Julia and Rose would continue their work as Underground Heroes, separate from their child. While Nico was apprehensive, wanting to stay with them as long as they could, it was inevitable.

... They had to be kept secret.

Nico had also gotten better, credit to their fast healing properties. The hero exams came and went, thankfully after the fact. They tried to enter the Underground Hero program, which they were really invested in. When the results came out, most of them managed to get in! Some others went into other hero agencies, but the rest pursued this new adventure.

Now, they were under King Cook's opposite, Mr. Cook's agency. The two were very different from each other. While the two's abilities were the same, as they both own the Darkness power, they use it in different ways. King Cook took over the Darklands and attempted to take every single place, only being stopped by the efforts of Julia and Rose, who had to go back in time to do so, which was a plan by...

Mr. Cook. He tries not to use his power all that often, keen on simply watching everyone else give their all. The underground hero knew the strength packed behind it. Nico didn't know what to feel about him at first, but once they could tell he was different, they were more motivated to start their missions.

The tenor's first encounter of the year however, was... *eventful.*

Their powers had been disabled by an enemy ambush, which left them vulnerable. Nico tried to retaliate, but was met with their face being pressed into the ground.

"I give up! Come on, that's too much for me to handle!" They exclaimed, squirming around under the person.

"You have to be prepared for every single situation!" They protested back, but eventually got off of Nico, who dusted themselves off.

"Not everyone is going to know Piccolo Style, mom!"

"What if they use a power stealing device? Be on guard at all times, Nico!" This person was not Julia, but yet another motherly figure to the tenor. Hannah is a section leader, specifically over the flutes. She mastered Flute Style, and started developing the fundamentals to Piccolo Style recently.

Flute Style was the art of taking down your enemy with quick, precise strikes, and as fast as possible. Piccolo Style was the same thing, except with the added ability to disable powers for a few moments. It was a very effective form of Instrument Combat.

Hannah is maybe an inch taller than Julia, with long brown hair. She's a very driven and protective person. Even with the multitude of other examples, she stands out as the most reliable in a pinch. Hero work is extremely time demanding, and Mr. Cook not appreciating the efforts of the flutes at all doesn't help their case. At face value, yes, heroes are all equal. But, Underground Hero work is even harder, case and point there's a lot of leeway with the concept of 'absolute secrecy.' While he states there's a lack of leadership in their section it's actually quite the opposite.

Nico groaned, rolling their eyes.

"Whatever, mom. I'm going to hang out with some of my friends." Hannah waved them off, the two sharing goodbyes.

For their first year, it was pretty underwhelming. Well, aside from the rigorous training they referred to as 'Camp.' Rookie Camp, pretty easy. You get to know the section leaders and drum majors and go over basic rudimentary stuff. The hard part of it was the Hero Exams, which was a relief...for only a few months.

Then there was the actual Hero Camp. 13 hours a day in two weeks spent just training in the hot July sun. Hard training too. While this was the norm in every program, the Underground Hero program was known for its extreme conditionings. While they heard stories about it from the leaders, they didn't know it was actually that hard. It was easier to bond with others though, so that's one plus out of a thousand negatives.

Some of their new friends had built strong bonds with them with what they had to go through, in the combined hero training they had. It involved pushing heavy props up and down the hill next to the base. Referred to as 'wagons,' they had a surprising amount of weight to them.

Windy, their best friend, also played tenor. The two got along really well as soon as they met. Her power was Impersonation. In a sense, she could exactly copy someone's appearance and voice, but not their powers.

After a few tries, Nico learned how to use her power, transforming into Mr. Cook. While they could only hold the form for a minute, a new thought arose. In theory, with their own ability to use anyone's power, and now the ability to copy anyone's appearance, this could very well work with their special missions.

As a great training opportunity, Nico tried out for drum major their freshman year. After all, Julia and Rose were 'graduating' and had been the drum majors that year also. Might as well give it a shot, though Nico was no match to the ones who had already tried countless times before, perfecting the fighting styles. It was impressive...but was it worth it if you didn't get it?

During the training, which took place in March, Nico and a friend of theirs went out just exploring C Town. Niles was a freshman too, and they were both trying out for the same position, so they gravitated towards each other. He was really good at Clarinet Style, but Nico wasn't sure if he even learned the other ones yet. One thing they did know for sure is that they were both fans of heroes.

"Thoughts on that new guy with the ice power? I thought he was pretty cool." Nico asked. There was a viral video going around the world about a new hero defeating a villain by freezing them to near death. Brutal.

"Not anything special, really. There's probably a lot of people out there that could pack him up."

"Now that I think about it, yeah." They kept talking about it until they heard screams coming from straight down in front of them. Nico and Niles looked at each other until the former got an alert on their watch. *Building fire a mile ahead. Amount involved unknown. Proceed with caution.* "Come on, let's go! Meet me at the convenience store nearby!" He nodded, and they ran off in the direction of the building.

....

Using their faster speed, Nico easily got everyone from the first few floors out of there, with Niles helping them with directions. The fire got worse higher up, and it was almost impossible for them to get near anyone with the flames roaring. It sparked up their flashbacks...they took in a deep breath and closed their eyes.

Imagine a cold, chilling breath coming out of my body. It's cold enough to get rid of the flames, but warm enough to not freeze anything over. Just for now though.

Sure enough, they let it out with all their might, and took out all of the flames. Nico sighed out of relief, then went towards one of the people and hoisted them over their shoulder. "Alright. Let's get you all out of here."

....

The flames were taken out, and so were all the civilians. Since the convenience store was to the back of the building, Nico opted to hop out of one of the back windows and wait there. What they didn't know was that it was going to take Niles awhile to get there, because the media piled up outside the front where he was.

"Incredible! This young man right here just saved the lives of countless people by evacuating all of them and extinguishing the flames!" What seemed like thousands of reporters and cameras swarmed and surrounded him. "This is the power and the hope for the new generation of heroes! Any words for those watching?" Millions of questions came his way, but he could only hear the voice of one.

"Follow your dreams."

....

Eventually, the year went by, and they had another round of Hero Camp. It was cut short, though, due to a villain attack and the security concerns from it. It was too bad...

The tenor was under Victor's division, the saxes. He was very surprised to see that Nico had already learned Sax Style and could already use it well. Now mastering all of the styles, he was now a Drum Major, but still took charge due to the absence of a saxophone section leader. Where did he go…?

The low reeds didn't have an actual group, but they all listened to Tag, the originator of Bari Style. The style is the same concept as Sax Style, but using your legs. It was seen as a breakthrough revelation, even though something like that would've been thought of earlier. Speaking of Bari Style, Chloe has been searching for Brandon and Mandy frequently during her off time. Since Nico believed they would come back on their own accord and didn't want to join her, along with her absence from their life, they started to slowly drift apart from each other. They were still friends, just not as close as they used to. Normal with kids their age.

"Tag doesn't want to be here. Tag's leaving." The aforementioned genius said, walking away immediately after Victor mentioned a mission assignment. Tag is a tall man with square glasses and curly black hair. He hardly is ever around, specifically if it involves some kind of work. He's known for doing 'whatever the hell he wants to do.' Tag is often seen working at his store, *Tag's School Supplies*. He gets a lot of orders from heroes, primarily the over achiever teenagers in their own program. Vic sighed. He's been doing that more often, thanks to him being in the Section Leader position for two years, and now a Drum Major.

"…and he's gone. Timer?" He said, looking through the plans and positions of their mission. Vic has black hair. He himself does not have a power. In fact, a surprisingly high percentage of prominent figures in the program don't have one. He works a nondescript minimum wage job in relation to fast food and chicken, the paychecks for hero work not being enough apparently. Victor's often tired from work, impulsively replying 'My pleasure' as if he's still there…how haunting…the struggles of being tied to the government in everyday life.

"A new record of 1.3 seconds." Sid told him, taking out his own tracker. Sid had grown quite a bit over the summer, towering over the rest of them. He was a whole foot taller than poor old Nico over there, who hadn't grown since 5th grade, maybe.

"Don't worry about getting a replacement. I'm already three steps ahead of you." A figure came in, shadowed out by the sun. Judging by their voice, it was…

"Kylie! You have your own section to run! What did I tell you about coming around here?" Vic attempted to scold them. They ignored him completely.

Kylie is of average height, just the slightest bit shorter than Victor, with her recently dyed black. They're the Mellophone section leader, who also plays saxophone, the same as Nico. They also work at that same job related to fast food and chicken. That's surprising, given their attendance rates and possible criminal background. They must not do background checks or something. Kylie hates the government, which is ironic because they basically spend their entire day working for them. Almost everyone with a leadership position in the program works there. Must be a requirement, or something…

"Anyways, Matt, what do you have planned after this mission?" They asked the other section leader, despite Vic's insistence to keep order.

"Oh. Nothing, really." Despite popular belief, Matt does not work at the non descript fast food place relating to chicken. He works at a nondescript music store somewhere in the city. Being at the beck and call of music related industries all the time is sad and unfortunate. He's frequently seen hanging around Kylie as they are best friends. Unlike them, he does not get persecuted for missing school. He is on thin ice though. 'Guilty by association' is a real thing sometimes.

He was the assistant Section Leader of the Saxes. He

had the title, but didn't have the power to reign in the section itself in their eyes, so not much gets done. They do see him as the actual leader though, with the main one being missing in action.

"Let's go steal some signs from the street later. I hear the politician they're advertising is a real menace to society!" The excuse for their frequent vandalism crimes is labelling the reason they steal specific signs as that 'they danger society.' True of all accounts, but not in the state government eyes.

"Sounds fun!" Matt replied.

"Whoa, whoa. Hold up! Don't you realize who you're discussing criminal activity in front of?"

"Your family is a long line of government officials, yeah, I know. At this point, I should be serving a life in prison for the amount of things I've said in front of you, but here I am, a professional underground hero."

"I think it would be more effective if *I* told them abou-"

"Be quiet Sid!" The two both told them. One thing that they collectively agreed upon is how they felt about Sid. Annoyance. Hardly any of the section leaders had powers, but were extremely strong in their own right, who gave inspiration to a lot of people.

"Let's just get out of here already and do the mission."

. . . .

The mission itself wasn't hard. It was just reconnaissance. There were various reports of a bunch of hooded figures trying to recruit others into their 'group.' They're often referred to as the 'Hive Mind,' as they all have similar behaviors, almost completely the same across all of the members who have been seen. None have been caught, and the place they were investigating was the suspected hideout of them.

One of the reasons why they were chosen was because rumors were going around about the Hive Mind existing in their very own hero program. Of course, there were doubts but nothing was disproving it either. Hannah, the head mission specialist, assigned the Saxophone section because 'the list of people that were primarily suspected had little to no one in their group.'

In the warehouse, there was barely anything there that gave any hints or clues. *Either this was a dead trail or they are pretty good at cleaning up, Victor wrote down in his report, as there were no guards, no weapons, not even a pen or paper could be found here. The place itself looks as if it hadn't been touched in decades. The problem is that inside of the place there was a fire that had just gone out recently, meaning some activity is here. Maybe it's not the type we're looking for. It's more likely we scared either homeless people or some reckless teenagers off.*

"Nico, go bring this to Hannah or someone else." He finished writing and handed it off to the young hero. They smiled, giving him a salute.

"Of course! See you tomorrow!" Vic rolled his eyes, watching them fly off in the direction of the school. As they jumped on trees for momentum, Nico thought of who would be the closest.

"Huh...Julia is usually doing her own missions, and same with Rose. I guess I won't see them for a bit." Their least favorite thing about her life as a hero is their limited contact with their parents. Thankfully Hannah was in the picture as her guardian. Speaking of her, they could probably find out where the flutes are and give it to her that way. "Nicole and Gracie interact with her the most, so if I could just find them..."

Nicole and Gracie were their friends, both of them in the flute section and a year older than them. They were kind of similar physically, but Nicole was more reserved than Gracie's outgoing personality. The former was shorter with slightly darker hair then the former. Nicole was the official librarian, knowledgeable on just about any topic, keeping records on every mission, person, or power they've encountered. While she preferred to stay out of battles as much as possible, Gracie was the complete opposite.

With lack of a better term, she was often described as explosive, taking all situations head on, but with expertise. Her water ability was nothing to sneeze at, which held Nico's attention at every single training match she saw her in. Gracie stands firm in her beliefs, not changing for anyone. Strong willed, gutsy, and other words similar fit her well.

At least, that's how you could describe her a year ago, when Nico first met her. As of recently, that spunk had been slowly falling apart, piece by piece, agonizingly slow. It seems only they knew why...but that's not the matter at hand. Nico needed to get this report to one of them.

Hannah's whereabouts were untraceable. It was almost like she was everywhere at once, usually handling stuff she wanted to do and not what she was ordered. Sometimes, Mr. Cook would get onto her for saving cats out of trees instead of her actual job. He must not understand that duty calls.

Nicole was usually found in the Underground Reserves, where all of the records are stored. Or she'd be somewhere with Gracie, who basically acts as spontaneously as Hannah.

Before they knew it, Nico was already landing on a tree above the base. They squinted, seeing two figures emerge from the extremely hidden hatch in the grass. *"Oh, that's where it was...I guess it was obvious."* Nico didn't want to scare them, so they just waited a bit. They hated eavesdropping, but it was better to not risk getting sucker punched by Gracie. Or either of them, actually. Nicole is probably stronger than she pretends to be.

"Yeah, he's always been leaving earlier than he used to. Should I be worried about it?"

"What kind of question is that? Of course you should. I know you trust him, but you have to be more careful. The investigation going on is a serious deal and we don't know who exactly is a part of that group." She responded genuinely. Gracie thought about it for a bit, but then…

"No way! He'd never do something like that. You're funny, Nicole." She busted out laughing, playfully hitting her shoulder.

"…It wasn't a joke. Please be more careful."

"Don't sweat it! I think we'll be alright." Sensing… awkward energy from Nicole, Nico finally decided to touch down when they reached the front of the base, approaching them from the front. Nicole felt relieved at their presence.

"Hey Nico. What brings you here?"

"Oh, hey guys! This is just a message report. Can one of you guys do me a favor and give it to Hannah for me?" They handed it to Gracie.

"I got it, now hurry and get home! It's getting late out." Nights in August weren't exactly the best. It was…humid outside. Gross.

"Alright then. See you guys soon!"

....

Eventually, Nico got home. Not where she lived with Hannah, but where Julia and Rose lived. They took some time off the year to spend time with each other, and Hannah was glad to let them have family bonding time. But this time, it was special. They were on paid leave for a weeklong break, and they would be taking a vacation to a place well known for its beautiful, pristine, crystal clear waters starting tomorrow. What sold it for Rose was the fact that people involved in hero work get discounts and secluded times on the beach.

"Hey, mom. Can we go on a vacation together? I know you're busy with hero work and stuff but I want to spend time with you and Rose." Nico said, approaching her while she was at her desk. This was a few months ago, their last visit with them. Julia gave her a sincere smile.

"Of course. I'm game whenever, and I'm sure Rose would love to hear that even more than I would. How does the beach sound?" She told them, and they went onto planning. When they told Rose, they were sure she almost started tearing up, but she was too heroic to do stuff like that.

．．．．．．．．．．．．

Nico sat down on a towel, watching Julia and Rose play fight in the water. Well, their 'play' fighting was brutal. Nico touches their own face, and it stung, because when Rose found out that they had buried her in sand during her nap, she tried throwing the container they used at Julia. But with the sand in her eyes, her direction missed, and hit their kid straight in the face. This is what led to their battle on public property.

"Mom, it's okay! I forgive Rose!" They tried shouting out to her. Julia already had her partner in an armlock...

"I don't!" She replied back, and despite their size difference, threw her straight into the water. Rose bounced up at her and they wrestled even more with each other. This clash would probably go on forever if they weren't broken up.

"Come on, please stop fighting for a second! Look at the sunset!" They stopped for a bit to look at where Nico pointed out, and yes, the sunset was beautiful. Reds, purples, and blues mixed and blended with each other thanks to the clouds. "Now apologize to each other." Julia and Rose shamefully met each other's gaze.

"...I'm sorry for throwing a bucket at our kid."

"...I'm sorry for beating you up."

"See? That wasn't hard, was it?" Nico asked them as they walked back to where they were sitting.

"Yeah, it was." Julia punched her in the shoulder.

"Cut it out!" They all laughed together, as they just chilled in the sand and watched the sun. Soon after they had to leave, so they went right into their hotel that was close to the beach. Nico jumped face first onto the bed, reveling in its softness.

"So, what's your guys' opinion on the investigation?" It was a great talking point to break the silence. After all, they were the ones who discovered the Hive Mind's existence.

It was almost coincidental. Before the castle disappeared a few days after the Ideal Reality's end, they searched it completely. While they didn't find anything completely incriminating, they found a symbol drawn on the ground. A hexagonal honeycomb, with candles that were blown out recently. Immediately, they reported it to Mr. Cook. After they had a meeting with him about trying to uncover their identities, Julia sighed...

"I guess this has layers to it."

...Their mission had to continue. It wasn't over.

"It's not surprising that there's corruption in the program, but this could end badly. Our identities could be exposed, potentially bringing danger to us. After all, the general public not knowing about us is a good thing. We're supposed to act in the shadows, so the evil in the world won't have a single clue about who we really are." Julia said first. "The ones among us went on to become actual heroes, technically starting there since no one knew about them prior. With this cult group on the other hand, we might have a greater risk of being attacked if people find out about the specific things we solved. Then again, it's the existence of the Hive Mind itself that's got me stuck. Why were they recruited into the Underground Hero program in the first place?" She was about to go onto a tangent, until Rose butted in.

"I've always been suspicious of certain people. Sure, people like Kylie and Tag get arrested for petty crimes, but there are numerous records of people in the program getting away with things like physical assault. Mr. Cook let it slide. I thought it was a product of the Ideal Reality, but I remember him saying something like, 'While there are some things that are inexcusable, this is another story. They had a bad day, and this will never happen again. They will be met with some punishment.'" She added on, attempting to copy his voice.

"I believe that we should all be cautious. This is especially for you, Nico. After all, we don't know their motives, their hideout, or even a single clue of their true identities." Julia warned them, sitting down next to them, Rose doing the same. The previous head drum major held Nico's hand, smiling at them. "But don't worry. As long as we're breathing, we'll have your back and come to your rescue. Isn't that right, Rose...?" After hesitating a bit, she took their hand too.

"Y-Yeah. No matter what."

"...Wow. Thanks, guys. I'm glad that you're my parents."

....

A month passed since they searched the warehouse. This day was a day off, to the appreciation of everyone. School had just begun the week before, which meant that Nico had to go back to living with Hannah. All good things come to an end, but she herself wasn't a bad thing. They just wanted to be with Julia and Rose forever, but it just wasn't possible since they're supposed to be a secret. No matter. Nico could still call them...which they did.

"I need to go back to running errands. I'll call you back tomorrow, okay? I promise," Julia told her kid over the phone. Nico was sitting on the couch, working out some minor homework assignments they got.

"Okay." The two shared goodbyes, and Nico ended the call. Right when they finished the last assignment, Hannah walked in the front door, locking it behind her. She had been planning out potential missions for the next few weeks with Mr. Cook, which took all night. Nico got up from the couch and walked towards her.

"I'm home! How was your first few days of school?" She asked them, both sharing a hug. Nico pulled back.

"Pretty good. My teachers are nice, and I made a new friend!"

"Really? What's their name?"

"His name is Niko. We have a few classes together, and he's super cool." Nico went on to tell her how he was a part of the Underground Hero program last year, but had quit to pursue his passion in art. His power was being able to draw anything and have it come to life. Hannah nodded along, invested with what they were telling her. "Anyway, one of my friends wants to meet me at the bookstore in thirty minutes. I'll call you on the way back!" They put on a rain jacket, since it was forecast to rain that day. Nico was meeting with Gracie to find a good story to read. Maybe they'll find something new.

"Have fun and be safe!"

....

"...This one is about heroes involved in a gambling ring with villains."

"I'll take that one." Nico immediately replied, taking

the book that Gracie was pointing at off the shelf. She pointed at another one.

"That one is about these teenagers who go into a TV and use their alter egos to fight."

"And that one."

"Pirates who travel the world in search of this grand treasure."

"Have it already."

"Idols that are training to perform in a grand competition."

"All of the movies, cards, books, episodes. Except for season two of the second series. It all went downhill after episode five. Haven't I told you about this series before," they replied, picking it up anyway. "I'll take another copy, though." They went to check out their books, left the store, and found a table at a restaurant to eat at. Nothing major, since neither of them make a suitable income for a fancy one. The two went through a bunch of conversation topics. Talking about different things they had been up to from the last time they saw each other. Gracie talked about the different missions that her section was sent on, and how little she got a chance to fight since Hannah always beat them down in seconds when she was there. The younger girl's power was nothing to sneeze at either. With the power of water, she's got control of a very abundant element in the world. She gets a lot stronger and even restless when the full moon comes up, probably because the moon has control over the waves of water. That was at least Nico's hypothesis.

"Can you believe she told me that? He wouldn't even think to do something like that!" Gracie complained, referring to what Nicole told her a month ago. Nico had listened to her explain the situation, even though they heard their conversation already…

"I see where you're coming from, but Nicole is right.

We don't know who is a part of the Hive Mind, and we have to be careful. You or me could be an accomplice and not even know about it." They replied, giving their thoughts. "Don't think of this as her hating him or something like that. She cares about you and only wants the best for you."

"...Do you think he's really a part of the Hive Mind?" Nico had to think about what to say. Apparently, other people had agreed with Nicole too when she told them about what she said. That included Hannah, who lives with Nico. They didn't want Gracie to think she said anything about it, but she never would've done something like that.

"I don't know. You just have to trust them and be careful. If you notice anything, minor or major, make sure to tell someone." They didn't want to say too much. After all, Hannah had left a possible suspect list on her desk one day and Nico saw basically every person he was friends with on there. They knew there was no virtual way possible for Nicole to get her hands on it too, but she watches everything. If anyone were to give a concrete analysis with just visuals alone, it would be her.

"Thanks for listening to me. Alright, how about we get back on track to that one episode?"

....

They parted ways a few hours later, and Nico decided to take the fastest route home. Books and discs in hand, they jumped through the forest. They were on the phone with Hannah.

"How close are you?"

"Not that far, I'm about halfway there now."

"Okay. I'll see you soon."

"Right." Suddenly Nico saw three figures approaching them from different directions. Putting their phone in their pocket, they dropped down to the ground, quickly surrounded by them. One of them was the same height as they were, but the rest were taller. "Now what would you guys want from me?"

"That's none of your concern. Just surrender to us." The one directly in front of Nico replied. They faintly could hear the cracking of electricity. Must be from the rain.

"No chance. Go find someone else to creep out." They just wanted to get out of the situation as quickly as possible. Maybe they should make a scanning power to figure out what their powers were. It's too risky to fight now without knowing. The person in front of them sighed.

"You leave us no choice. Do it." Before Nico could do anything, they felt something invade their nervous system, leaving them unable to move. Not even speak. At first, they tried pumping their body full of the energy they were holding back to try and break loose, but it was fruitless. What was like an electric shock coursed through them a few times, and even when Nico regained control over their body, they wouldn't be able to move without recovering first.

They wasted no time.

The one to the right of Nico punched them in the face. It wouldn't have hurt if it was just a normal hit, but it was charged with even more electricity. They quickly felt their right eye swelling up, and felt their body slowly collapsing. Nico retaliated by firing a blast at them, knocking them into a tree. For extra measure, they blew ice onto them, sticking them onto the tree. The tenor backed away from the other two.

"Pulling cheap tricks to win, huh? That won't do anyone good." Nico told them, stuttering heavily, when they suddenly felt the invasion again. The smaller one didn't move, but the one they assumed was the boss kicked them in the right side. Nico felt something break, their body screaming in pain. They grunted at most, not wanting them to feel any victory. Right when the smaller one moved, Nico broke free, which must be their weakness. They disregarded the pain for now, using their other leg to push off of and grab the person's face. "So it's you huh? Using cheap tricks? You'll regret it."

Squeezing, they cracked something beneath the hood but otherwise couldn't get it off. Using the now heavy weight of their right leg, Nico put all of the energy they had left in it to knee them in the stomach, then tossed them over to the other one they knocked out. All of the electricity had slowed them down severely, so they didn't notice when the 'boss' reeled back...and kicked them in the side again. Nico dropped to the wet ground, kind of glad they remembered to wear a rain jacket.

Any positive thoughts flew out the window right when a hard stomp was dealt to their stomach. Nico nearly blacked out just from that, but then another came...and another...and another...They wanted to fight back, but they couldn't even bring their body to move an inch.

"Hold it there! I'm seeing eight enemy forces approach us now! We have to get out of here!" The smaller one shouted, picking up the one Nico knocked into a tree. With one last stomp, the bigger one nodded and followed close after them. They got out of there so quickly that the 'enemy forces' hadn't even got there yet. That group must be extra careful to not be caught.

Nico tried pushing energy through their body, but the points where there was excessive force was blocked off.

I guess I'll just use my arm. Even their thoughts were in stutters. They could feel an adrenaline rush course through, so they used the extra energy to push themself up. No matter what, they couldn't move their right leg, so it dragged against the ground. The trees made it hard to see, and the rain wasn't making it any better. Before they could make a single step, a huge object was suddenly in front of them. It turned on its blinding lights, so now Nico could tell it was a vehicle. They stood like a deer in headlights, not being able to move any further.

...They heard a loud noise.

....

"You guys, follow after them and don't stop until you capture them! Victor, you stay here with me. I'm gonna need help getting them to the hospital." They heard a voice distant, yet close. They felt their body being gently picked up, which hurt a lot. A whole lot. They couldn't bring themselves to voice the pain. "Nico, are you alright? It's me, Hannah. Stay with me." They could barely bring themself to respond.

"...okay." Nico saw double, before their eyes blacked out completely. Sleep felt nice, even more than before.

"You've got to stay awake. Don't close your..." Her voice got farther and farther away until they heard nothing...

. . .

. . .

...All of the hero stories that I've seen tell happy tales of a perfect story and perfect ending. They all lived happily after, never seeing death until complications from old age. They became household names, living on even after death in the form of a legacy...

. . .

. . .

...Except for mine.

. . .

...Why me?

AVAILABLE NOW!

DON'T MISS OUT ON THESE RELEASES BY
MADISON PATE

AVAILABLE WHEREVER BOOKS ARE SOLD

Amazon, Books-A-Million, Barnes & Noble, Etc.

WWW.TANDJPUBLISHERS.COM

www.ingramcontent.com/pod-product-compliance
Lightning Source LLC
Chambersburg PA
CBHW021952170726
47994CB00020B/217